SU

"Rush 'em!" their chief was commanding. "C'mon, you lazy bastards, wipe 'em out!"

A man scurrying by Jessie's window abruptly let out a cry and clawed at his chest, spurting blood on his calfskin vest.

As dawn began to ooze across the eastern horizon, some of the shooting slowly died away and an eerie silence held the camp.

"They got one more stab, I judge," Rod Delmonico growled.

"Speak of the devil," Opal snapped. "Here they come!"

WESLEY ELLIS

LONE STAR

AND THE TRAPPER TURF WAR

J

JOVE BOOKS, NEW YORK

LONE STAR AND THE TRAPPER TURF WAR

A Jove Book / published by arrangement with
the author

PRINTING HISTORY
Jove edition / October 1994

ISBN: 0-515-11477-4

A JOVE BOOK®
Jove Books are published by The Berkley Publishing Group,
200 Madison Avenue, New York, New York 10016.
JOVE and the "J" design are trademarks
belonging to Jove Publications, Inc.

PRINTED IN THE UNITED STATES OF AMERICA

10 9 8 7 6 5 4 3 2 1

Chapter 1

Sometimes getting there is half the danger.

Southeastward from Seattle, beyond the coastal plain, the foothills rising to the Cascade Range and Mount Rainier formed a remote country of steepening culverts and ridge-flanking woods, flexing toward increasingly savage heights of staggered slopes, creek-bottom gulches, and dense stands of timber. It was perilous country, a devilishly harsh land that seemed forbidding . . . and foreboding. Evil seemed to brood in the rain that soaked the land by day, and to lurk in the deep shadows of the overcast night. Settlers and encampments were few and far between, as much at risk as errant travelers to the roving bands of bandits and bloodthirsty renegades who hid out up in the isolated reaches. And yet, although men were consistently killed, their lives snuffed out by the silent knife and the bushwhack bullet, more men kept pushing into these uplands, fighting for a toehold in the timber industry as lumberjacks and in sawmills to supply the lucrative Seattle and Tacoma markets.

At the moment, Jessica Starbuck and her partner, Ki, were pushing into the uplands. Aware of the risks, they rode warily, if wearily. Remaining carefully alert was difficult, for rarely had they trekked along a more monotonous wagon road, with no sounds to accompany them other than those of birds and small game, the muffled swishing through forest groves, shod hooves clopping over rock and gravel, and every so often the splash of rushing water from nearby Puyallup River, which the road more or less paralleled. Yesterday they'd ridden the Northern Pacific coach south from Seattle to the crossroads town named Puyallup, where they'd spent the night in a railroad hotel. In the gray of a morning drizzle, they'd bought a pair of sturdy horses at the local livery stable and began their day's journey to Orting, a junction where the Carbon River flowed into the Puyallup. Around midmorning, the drizzle lifted and the clouds tapered off, leaving a bright spring day that was now warming the riders and drawing steam from the sunlit roadbed.

Squinting from under her flat-crowned Stetson, Jessie rode her mouse-colored dun mare manstyle, not "ladylike" on a tortuous sidesaddle perch. She was clad casually in jeans, denim jacket, and chambray shirt, which did little to conceal her firm, jutting breasts and sensuously rounded thighs and buttocks. Her mother had been a redheaded beauty who'd passed to her daughter a long-limbed, lushly molded figure, flawless ivory skin, and a cameo-like face with a pert nose and a spark of feline audacity to the wide-set, golden-green eyes. And Jessie's father, Alex Starbuck, had given a steadfastness to her dimpled chin and a shrewd if sometimes humorous twist to her lips. Even though both parents were dead—murdered and subsequently avenged—in a quite real sense they lived on, embodied in the spirit and actions of their offspring. And Jessie had every intention of staying alive: her derringer lay concealed behind the wide square buckle of her belt, and her shellbelt and holster looped over the horn of her stock saddle, so her custom Colt revolver wouldn't chafe her thigh but would be within easy reach.

Ever vigilant, Ki sat erect astride his tough roan gelding, a lithe man in his early thirties whose features bore the handsome quality that appeals to women who like their men tempered by experience and bronzed by the sun. Like Jessie, he was dressed in normal range garb—faded jeans, loose-fitting collarless shirt, worn black vest, and battered hat. His feet were clad in Asian-style rope-soled cloth slippers, but in a land of Indian moccasins, these were not remarkable. Nor were his almond-shaped eyes, straight blue-black hair, and the golden color of his skin, which strongly suggested that his mother had been Japanese and his father a white American. In this Pacific Coast Territory of varied blood and race, interracial relationships were too common to draw attention.

Ki and Jessie had known each other since childhood, when her father—head of a worldwide entrepreneurial empire—had hired Ki to be Jessie's companion and guardian. It had been a wise choice, for Ki, as an orphaned half-breed outcast in Japan, had been apprenticed to one of the last great samurai, and had grown skilled in unarmed combat as well as in the use of bow and arrow, sword, staff, stick, and throwing weapons. Indeed, even now in his vest and pockets were stashed short daggers and other small throwing weapons, including a supply of *shuriken*: little razor-sharp steel disks shaped like six-pointed stars. Devoted to Jessie and loyal to her far-flung inherited interests, Ki was to a great degree the protector behind the Starbuck throne. But to Jessie, he was as close, and as much an equal, as if he were her blood brother.

"Very curious," she remarked idly to Ki as they jogged along. "A very curious mission this is, just as I told Val Gresham when he brought it up. Wonder just what it is that this timberman, this Rod Delmonico, couldn't be more specific about with Gresham." She fell silent, recalling what Valentine Gresham, Starbuck field representative for western Washington, had reported to her when she and Ki had visited his office in Seattle. That had been two days before, when they had returned from troubleshooting a salmon cannery operation up in Alaska. Initially, her plans had been to pay a courtesy call on Gresham, sleep over, then return to Starbuck headquarters back on her large Circle Star ranch in Texas. But what

Gresham had to tell her had changed all that.

"As you know, Miss Starbuck," the field agent had said, "ordinarily, when any of our subsidiaries or investment properties has trouble, the owner or manager isn't backward about speaking right out, telling what's bothering him, and telling us to get busy—just how, too, like as not."

"So I take it this Delmonico you speak of was rather . . . well, vague?" Jessie had asked.

"Vague?" Gresham had laughed once, sharply. "Why, that's no word for it. Delmonico was downright tight-lipped and mysterious about everything. Most he'd say was that he wouldn't tell anybody anything till a Starbucker I personally vouched for showed up at his lumber camp outside Zenobia. Then he'd explain the situation, whatever it is, and they could make their own plans. What beats me, Miss Starbuck, is that he ever called on us at all. His ol' ma—er, his father, Osgood Delmonico, he's the one Starbuck financed to buy the timber rights to the surrounding hills. Anyway, Osgood always bragged he could take care of himself and his holdings. He did, too, and after he passed away, his son and daughter have proven to be chips off the same stubborn log . . ."

Mulling over that point, Jessie commented to Ki, "Rod Delmonico and his sister made it plain that they didn't want or need anybody's help. Until now. Now, apparently, Rod is demanding help, no questions asked."

"Likely someone's playing around in his preserves," Ki responded with his characteristic dry grin. "Somebody he can't lay his finger on. So he thinks he might as well get something for the payments he makes to Starbuck."

"I've a suspicion it must be pretty serious, if Val Gresham is right about the Delmonico offspring inheriting their father's obstinacy. Osgood was a pioneer in this region, put together a tract of thousands of acres by sheer dint of will, and became what some folks call a timber baron. He and his crews fought their own battles, and it appears that hasn't changed. So something mighty odd must've happened; otherwise, a Delmonico never would've called on Starbuck for help."

"And you mean to find out what."

"That's right, Ki. After we visit a man even more contrary."

"Quinn Abbott."

Jessie nodded. When first hearing of Rod Delmonico's urgent plea, Jessie had figured that Gresham could handle matters without her intervention and that there'd be no need for her to delay heading back to Texas. Then Gresham had mentioned news—more a bit of business gossip than fact—concerning Quinn Abbott, the ornery owner of the Flaming Geyser Stage & Freight Line.

"I've kept tabs on Abbott, just as you wanted," Gresham had told Jessie. "Well, rumor has it that he's finally bitten off more than he can chew; short of a miracle, he's going belly-up."

"Sorry to hear it." And Jessie meant it. A decade before, Quinn Abbott had given refuge to her father at great personal risk, without question or compensation, saving him from the enemies who were hunting him down. Alex Starbuck had never been able to repay Abbott; his every offer of help had been firmly declined, to put it mildly, Abbott refusing to be "beholden." Those offers had included one just three years before, for a loan to help Abbott purchase the stage and freight outfit. It operated in the area where Jessie and Ki were traveling now and was headquartered in the next town, Orting; if it had received sufficient capital, the line could have expanded rapidly to dominate most of Pierce County. But Abbott had rejected the funding. Instead, he'd mortgaged the line for a bank loan to make up the difference between his savings and the money needed to buy it. That was akin to shooting himself in the foot, but Abbott took a gambler's delight in operating on the narrowest possible margin and, when he got away with it, jeering at the wiseheads who had prophesied his ruin.

"But wasn't he doing well just six months ago?" Jessie had asked. "What could've affected a prosperous business so badly in so short a time?"

"Abbott's suffered a rash of lost cargoes, robbed passengers, beaten crews, and broken equipment," Gresham had answered, shaking his head. "He needs to borrow to replace equipment and hire more guards, but he's strained his credit to the breaking point with Puget Sound Trust and Savings, the only local bank who'd deal with him. If Puget Sound calls in his loan, it'll bring on a complete bust."

"Val, did you . . . ?"

"Yes, Miss Starbuck, I offered Abbott a credit line. No strings, not even any interest." Gresham had glanced hesitantly at Jessie. "I . . . I thought that's what you would've suggested if you'd been here."

"Yes, yes. And?"

"I won't repeat his reply. I can't. Let's just say it was 'no thanks' . . ."

Now, Jessie turned to Ki with a disgusted expression. "That irascible, blue-brained mule! Well, Quinn Abbott's met his match this time. My father never forgot a debt or a friend; neither do I. Abbott needs aid, and aid he's going to get, whether he likes it or not!" She shifted in her saddle to stare determinedly ahead. "He's what convinced me to stay hereabouts instead of heading back to the Circle Star right away. Orting is on the way to the Delmonico timber camp, and that's a coincidence I simply can't pass up. Abbott had better be there in Orting, too, operating his line the way he's supposed to be doing. And as soon as he agrees to spend enough Starbuck funds to get it back on its feet, we'll go on to the Delmonicos and see what all the mystery there is about. They won't waltz me around with vague answers, either—"

"Shh!"

Jessie's voice dropped to a whisper. "What is it? Hear something?"

"No."

"What do you mean, you—"

"I mean, I don't hear anything. And I should. Listen!" Ki urged intently, craning his neck to look around. "Jays that'd been squawking in the trees . . . where are they now? Nothing! Not a rustle in the underbrush, not a sign of even a squirrel. Nothing!"

Noting the silence, Jessie surveyed the terrain. They were riding across level, rocky woodlands here, approaching a narrow pass where boulders were piled high on either side. The pass appeared to be about a quarter mile in length; as they entered, Jessie inspected the jumbles of rocks for signs of ambush, but saw nothing to arouse her suspicions. And no rider was in sight behind or ahead of them on the twisting trail. She was studying the left side of the pass when a metal hornet suddenly buzzed past her, almost brushing against her shoulder. From downwind came the crack of a rifle.

"Into the rocks!" Jessie shouted. "Get out of sight!"

Ki jumped his horse aside and forward just as a second metal hornet flew past within a few feet of him. Scrambling for cover, he sprang from the saddle alongside Jessie, who snatched her gunbelt from the saddle horn and her carbine out of its saddleboot. Together, they flung themselves behind some protective boulders at the base of the hill. The two discharges echoed through the pass; Jessie thought the shots had been fired from high up on both sides, and risked peering up to see if she could tell.

The rifles cracked two more times. Chips of granite flew off the edge of the boulder, showering down her back, but now she was sure that the ambushers had them in a cross fire. She glanced across at Ki. "Why?"

"Why?" Ki looked at her as though she'd gone daft. "Why, to kill us, that's why!"

"Up ahead are a pair of bushwhackers—maybe more. But why? Nobody knows we're coming this way. So are they set up there waiting for anybody happening along, or did they mistake us for someone in particular?"

"Well, why don't we just head up thataway and ask them?" Ki said it with a hint of sarcasm, but he was serious, figuring that otherwise, the ambushers would simply stay put and wait them out. Cautiously, he began working his way up the bank, Jessie falling in behind him, darting from boulder to boulder, keeping as much as possible behind cover. In the silence, the least noise carried. Ki thought he heard a boot scrape rock, and tensed. But it was Jessie who first spied their enemy as, high on the slope on the other side of the pass, a figure dipped stealthily out from concealment and started toward a new position.

He never lived to reach it. Jessie's Winchester carbine bucked in her grasp, and the figure stiffened and sprawled out in the rocks.

Ki caught a muttered curse from the slope on their side. "You can't shoot up at that guy without showing yourself," he observed. "Cover me as best you can. I'll see if I can't prod him into moving."

Silent and motionless, Jessie waited and watched as Ki eased slowly to higher ground. The ambusher fired, his bullet answered by two fast slugs from Jessie while Ki, hunching low, continued working his way up the bank in a circuitous route. Underbrush covered the lower portion of the bank, joined higher up by a scattering of scraggly conifers. Ki didn't heistate when he reached the trees, but plunged on through shifting sunlight and shadows, the resinous scent of rain-washed fir about him. His padded footfalls were muffled by Jessie's carbine and the ambusher's rifle. Suddenly, the fringe of tress dropped away to a narrow pocket that ended at a lift of broken wall.

Again, Ki chose a roundabout course, darting across the pocket in a wide, concealing curve that left him better positioned to climb above and behind the ambusher without being spotted. He cautiously navigated the steep hillside, occasionally pausing to shade his eyes and study the lay of the rise, trying to ascend through the screening growths and raw crevices in a looping hairpin swing that would bring him to where he could get the drop on the man. Easier said than done! When he'd holed up in the rocks, the ambusher had picked his spot with deadly skill.

Rifle shots continued to be traded, a haze of smoke wafting from a ledge to his left and marking the ambusher's vantage point amid a crop of staggered rock slabs that cut off Ki's view of him. But that meant the man probably couldn't see Ki, either. As he climbed higher at an angle in order to approach the ledge from above, on the ambusher's blind side, Ki caught a glimpse of the ambusher's horse—which caused him some concern. For there were *two* horses ground-reined there, and he doubted mightily that the man Jessie had hit on the far bank would've left his mount over here. No, that extra horse indicated there were two men holed up over here, not one. The odds suddenly worsened by a hundred percent. And Ki, as usual, was not toting a gun. He disliked firearms as a rule, but he had to admit that when confronting two killers with guns, fisting some big-barreled, high-caliber revolver tended to be more intimidating than holding a dagger. Well, at this point he'd be damned if he was going to go back down and borrow Jessie's pistol. He'd just have to do with what he had, and hopefully capture them alive to answer Jessie's questions. But if it came down to kill or be killed, so be it.

First, though, he had to get to them.

Slowly, and very gently, he started across a short slide of loose shale and gravel. He was close, not more than twenty yards, yet the footing was treacherous. Despite his best efforts, he slipped and had to dig into the sliding rock to keep from falling, then lunge laterally across the slope to a pile of boulders, just as the sliding rock cascaded down.

The immediate aftermath of the fall was an eerie silence. Perhaps it was because Jessie and the men needed to reload, or someone was hit . . . but Ki had a sinking sensation that it was due to the noise of the rockfall. Time was of the essence now. He slithered higher in quick, snake-like moves, focusing intently, his nimble fingers touching the razor-edged throwing daggers tucked in his vest. Gliding around the back of a boulder with his body flat to the ground, he finally eased into position and stared over and downward.

Two men, all right. One, in cheap gray woolen pants and hickory-colored shirt, was behind a low jumble of rocks on a small ledge, crouching on one knee while sighting down a Spencer .56–.50 repeater, tensing, preparing to blast Jessie. His partner, dressed in old Army blues, was standing a couple of feet back, fidgeting with his rifle.

" . . . I tells yuh, Hank, I heard sumpthin' o'er thataway," the standing man was saying.

"You allus hear noises," Hank scoffed. "Ain't no way anybody could've gotten up here without us catchin' it. I see your noises, Gallager, I'll believe 'em."

"No harm in checking," Gallager retorted. "The stretch will do me good."

Rising while their backs were still to him, Ki ordered, "Drop them."

Gallager pivoted, firing as fast as he could lever.

He wasn't fast enough. Throwing a dagger with efficient dispatch, having no intention of making it a contest, Ki nailed the man deep in the base of his neck, the blade passing between vertebrae, slicing his spinal cord and bringing his misspent life to an end without so much as a whimper.

"Drop it!" Ki snapped at the crouching Hank. "Don't move!"

Hank was no smarter than his partner. Jerking spasmodically around, gawking as Gallager toppled, he blurted, "Shit! I'll blow your head off!"

Ki nailed him in the chest.

Hank toppled awry with his leg bent under him, his rifle still gripped in one hand, the haft of the dagger protruding from his chest. Ki paused, ready to fling another dagger if need be. A noise behind him made him spin around, but it was only Jessie, scrambling up with her pistol held ready, relief welling in her eyes.

"Thank God," she sighed. "Is he . . . ?"

"Not yet, but he's not going to last."

Jessie, keeping her pistol trained, walked forward with Ki and stood over the prostrate, dying figure. "Why did you open fire on us?" she asked. "Mistake us for some other riders?"

"You . . . you're Starbuck, ain't you?" Hank gasped out.

"That's correct."

"No mistake, then."

"But why?" Jessie demanded. "Are you working for someone?"

"Yeah. We knowed you was comin' . . . an' . . . an' . . ." The man shuddered, his chest heaved once, and he expired, twitching a final, faint tattoo on the stony earth.

"Hell!" Disgusted, Jessie turned away.

Ki checked both bodies for identification or other clues, but came up with nothing. He then inspected their Spencers, but the repeaters were stock '65 Indian models without oddities or markings. He and Jessie clambered over the rocks to the ground-reined horses, hoping a brand or a saddlebag might hold a hint, but the brands were of cattle ranches far from the region and the saddlebags contained standard gear and foodstuffs. They spent the next hour hiking over to the other side of the pass to find the ambusher Jessie had shot, only to find that he was equally a stranger, his rifle and horse equally plain. All three horses they unsaddled and set loose, but left the dead men where they lay; at least as carrion, their otherwise useless lives would be worth something. When Jessie and Ki finally returned to their own mounts, the best they could conclude from their efforts was that the men were common gun-thugs, as unwashed and nondescript as their belongings.

Remounting, Jessie and Ki rode on slowly, watching carefully now as they went on through the pass and emerged into open meadowland. Perplexed, Jessie kept shaking her head. "I don't understand it. But some sort of plot must've been hatched to get us in that little pass before we could reach Orting and see Quinn Abbott."

"It doesn't have to be connected to Abbott," Ki pointed out. "It's just as likely, if not more so, that our welcoming party was to stop us before we could learn why Rod Delmonico called on Starbuck for help."

"Well, the one thing that seems clear, Ki, is that somebody besides Val Gresham knew we were coming. And nobody was supposed to."

★

Chapter 2

They reached Orting without further incident, save for a blustery cloudburst in the late afternoon. The sun broke out again, continuing its decline into evening as Jessie and Ki started down into the hill-hemmed river valley where Orting nestled. The rain had turned the roadbed into a ribbon of gumbo, forcing their horses to slow to a high-stepping walk. About midway, they passed a Flaming Geyser wagon and team struggling up the long grade with a full load of fresh-sawed lumber.

"What'n hell did they want to lay out the damned burg in a gulch for?" cussed the mud-spattered teamster, as Jessie and Ki ploughed by him.

The valley was hardly a gulch, but a wide flat, rich with grass, wildflowers, and groves of oaks and alders. Virtually in the middle of the valley, the

Carbon River flowed into the Puyallup, and there at the confluence was Orting, perched along the south bank of the Carbon. At a distance, the town did look like a burg—a motley hodgepodge of buildings, cabins, and shacks, most of them clustered near a pond, drying yard, and smoke-belching sawmill. The setting sun, casting fiery streamers over the hill they were descending, radiated steamy hues off of rooftops and windowpanes, making Orting appear to be sleepily ashimmer.

Indeed, as they crossed the wooden bridge over the Carbon and entered the outskirts of Orting, they saw that around the center of town were dwellings shuttered from the weather and low false-fronted buildings wrapped in growing shadows. Smack-dab central stood a weathered signpost with arrows that pointed in three directions: PUYALLUP, back the way they'd come; LAKE KAPOWSIN, straight on southward; and WILKESON, to the east up in the hills bordering Mount Rainier. A short ways along the route to Lake Kapowsin was a fenced yard roughly a block in size. Set by the front gates was a large, square cabin of whitewashed boards, on the door of which was painted:

FLAMING GEYSER STAGE & FREIGHT LINE
Yard Office * Please Enter

The gates were open, and as Jessie and Ki reined in by the office, they could see hostlers moving about the stock corrals and sagging, hip-roofed barns, while others were busy hitching teams and loading large freight wagons. The office door was also open, but lounging on the front stoop like a bored sentinel was a burly teamster, wolf-jawed with teeth to match, long-nosed and slit-eyed, armed with an old Starr .44 and an even older Whitney twenty-gauge, muzzle-loading shotgun.

Approaching him, Jessie asked, "Is Mr. Abbott in, please?"

He eyed her up and down like a beef carcass. "Who're you?"

"Starbuck," she answered, tersely now, but keeping control of her temper. "Miss Jessica Starbuck. He's expecting me."

With a grunt, the man went inside and shut the door. For a moment, they heard nothing. Then a rumbling bass voice roared forth: "Starbuck? Y'say she's expected? Here?" Whatever the answer was didn't carry outside, and for another minute all was quiet. Then: "Hell, Plumas! You rummy asshole, why didn't you say so? Show her in!"

Plumas came out, his wolf-jawed face a sullen red, his eyes casting Jessie a mighty hard glare. "Thought you told me the boss's expecting you."

"He is; he just didn't know it," Jessie replied sweetly, brushing past. Entering behind her, Ki flashed Plumas a bland smile and closed the door.

A hanging lantern cast smoky yellow light over several chairs, filing cabinets, bookcases, a wall map of the territory, and a battered oak desk near the one window. Directly under the lantern stood a rotund old man in a rumpled cutaway sackcloth suit, hands clasped behind his back, white whiskers padding his plump, grinning face.

"B'gawd, it is you!" he bellowed with recognition. "Li'l Jessica, all growed up—and Ki! What'n hades are you doing in this neck of the woods?"

"Passing through," Jessie replied warmly. "A bit of business up around Zenobia. And you, Mr. Abbott?"

"Quinn! You're old enough to use my first name."

"Very well, if you'll call me Jessie. So, Quinn, what're you doing? Or should I ask, *how* are you doing?"

"Aha! I get it now. Your white-livered, droopy-drawered coyote of an office manager done snitched on me!" Swallowing a juicy epithet, Abbott looked ready to bust a gut. Suddenly, deflating, he scratched his white hair and stepped to the wall map. "Wal, it ain't no secret, Jessie, not that anybody could ever keep one from you." His stubby finger pointed to Orting. "Here we is. This's my line's hub, with routes fanning out to terminals at Puyallup, Lake Kapowsin, and Wilkeson. I got the only service, too, runnin' everything from passengers to lumber, farm produce, mining—"

"Ore mining?" Jessie cut in. "There's gold or silver hereabouts?"

"North along the border there is, but not here. No, I mean coal. Just a little; not like the King County deposits on the western slopes of the Cascades, but enough for me to haul profitably. I make money okay, but I spend it. Just figure what the pay for the drivers, guards, hostlers, stablemen, blacksmiths, and station agents would be. Then add food cost for men at the stations, equipment, hay, feed for the animals—you've got a whoppin' big figure." Abbott turned from the map, moved to his desk. "So far, I've made a little more'n I've spent, what with income from mail contracts and whatnot. Now one section of the line has suddenly showed signs of collapsin'."

"Around here, at your hub?" Ki asked.

Abbott shook his head. "Nope, on the eastern route, from about midway to Wilkeson. And that leg is my most profitable, too, from constantly freightin' cargo up and logs down outta them timber camps. But things has got so bad that we can't keep to our schedules. The Post Office Department has warned that unless we do, we lose the mail franchise."

"What kind of things?"

"Just about every kind you can think of, Jessie. Coaches don't break down, seems like, unless they're somewhere between the relay station at South Prairie and the Wilkeson depot. Freight wagons don't fall off cliffs or catch fire anywhere else. Bandits cluster on that stretch of road like buzzards around a dead mule."

"Sounds like somebody wants to knock that section out of business," Jessie reckoned, "or you into bankruptcy. Any ideas who?"

"Northern Pacific."

Jessie was genuinely shocked. "The N.P.?"

"Don't use that tone of voice with me! It don't make no sense to me, neither."

"You're right, Quinn; it doesn't."

"Y'see, the railroad is set to build a spur line from Puyallup—wal, from Meeker, the next station, to be technical about it—all the way to Wilkeson. When it gets runnin', my outfit's a goner. There's no way I can fight it and win." Abbott settled into his desk chair, leaned back. "However, the N.P.'s offered to buy me out. For a damn—er, darn fair price, too. They figure it'll pay off, to get a ready-made setup for hauling construction needs, while continuing to run the line so's the customers stay happy. No fuss, no muss."

"Then accept the offer and be done," Jessie suggested.

"You betcha. But there's a complication. The N.P.'s long-range plan is to split the spur at Wilkeson, extend a track south into Mount Rainier country, and another track north to tie in with the proposed main line east across Snoqualmie Pass. Right now its right-of-ways are nothing but pack trails linking a handful of trading posts. The posts are controlled by two partners, Hugh Fitzpatrick and Urias Locke, who seem to be in plumb cozy cahoots with outlawry, and're suspected of dabblin' in a li'l thievin' and a li'l third-rate gunplay themselves. The railroad don't want to hafta hire an army to protect its crews, so . . ." Abbott lapsed into silence with a shrug.

"So Fitzpatrick and Locke are in on the deal," Jessie finished.

"A package deal. Now, as I say, p'raps them two ain't precisely choirboys, but they ain't got no reason to ruin me. They'd foul the deal. And if they wanted out of it, they'd just run."

Jessie frowned. "I've never heard of the N.P.

putting together something like this."

"It didn't, not directly. The deal was engineered by a certain Horace Mahoney, outta Tacoma. Shrewd li'l bast—broker, earnin' a percentage of the sales price for gettin' us all to agree. So I can't figure him as being behind my troubles, either, breakin' the golden egg he himself laid. Fact is, Mahoney's starin' at a loss right now." Rummaging through papers on his desk, Abbott swung around in his chair and handed Jessie a letter addressed to him and dated the previous week. It read:

> In regard to the option on Flaming Geyser Stage and Freight Line, which on behalf of Northern Pacific Railroad this firm was to take up on the 28th of this month, I will be unable to complete the sale at the negotiated price. As ascertained by the latest examination of your accounts, the returns on your line have fallen off drastically, due, I suppose, to inefficient management. The business reflects such a deficit that Northern Pacific can offer you only half of the price originally agreed upon, anticipating heavy expense to bring the line up to its proper capacity. Assuming you present yourself as arranged at the Puget Sound Trust & Savings in Puyallup on the 28th, I shall be honored to close the deal on that basis. I can give you no more time to consider the matter, as I am due elsewhere on the first.
>
> Y'r M'st Ob'd'nt S'rv'nt,
> T. Horace Mahoney

"This sure puts me in a bind," Abbott continued, as Jessie passed the letter to Ki. "I'm behind in my mortgage payments, but based on the option, the bank granted me an extension till month's end. The mortgage has a due-on-sale clause, y'see, which is why we'd agreed to meet at the bank. But I can't pay it off unless I get full price from Mahoney."

"Is the bank eager to foreclose?" Ki asked, returning the letter.

"They acted horrified at the prospect," Abbott replied glumly. "That's why I got my reprieve. If they do take over, they'll likely dump the line fast and cheap to Northern Pacific, which maybe gives the railroad a motive."

"Seems to me it'd want to keep the peace, to keep the line profitable."

"Well, then, Jessie, I don't know who wants to do me in or why!" Abbott snapped gruffly, combing his fingers through his hair. "To find out and put a stop to it, I swear I'd make a pact with the devil."

"But not with a Starbuck."

"I've been reluctant, true. But that tinhorn Gresham kept trying to give me money, just like your daddy did. I don't truck with givin' or bein' given. Besides, money ain't gonna save me at this point. I gotta get that section back to operatin', and that's gonna take wiping out a nestful of sidewindin' skunks pronto. And I ain't got the first notion where to begin."

"Well, we're heading up thataway," Jessie said noncommittally. "We'll keep our eyes peeled, maybe see what we can do."

"Oh, no, you don't! This ain't no game for a lady!"

"Any game a lady plays," Jessie argued, "is a lady's game."

"Poker ain't!" Abbott retorted. "This's what it is, cutthroat poker. And me holdin' a busted hand with no hope of bluffin'. Uppin' the bet would just be throwin' good chips after bad, Jessie, so thanks for offerin', but let it lay. In ten days, on the twenty-eighth, I'm foldin'."

With that, Abbott had explained his problems about as much as he wished to, and steered the conversation into more sociable small talk. Presently, it was time to say good-bye. He escorted Jessie and Ki to the door with warm regards, voicing his hope for another visit and apologizing for the condition of Orting's one hotel. His cheerful bellowing followed them to the street. They swung into their saddles and reined their horses around. Several yards up the street, Ki glanced back.

"Jessie," he said softly, "if I'm not mistaken, that Plumas gent was snuggling mighty close to the door, like he'd glued his ear to it."

"I noticed that, too." Jessie pursed her lips, then said thoughtfully, "Looks to me like Quinn is bucking something very big. Whoever's fighting him for as big a prize as control of Flaming Geyser won't let us get in their way if they can help it."

"Maybe they've tried to stop us already."

"If you're referring to the ambush, maybe so. . . . But that just raises the question of how they knew we were coming, when nobody, not even Quinn, was expecting us."

"Well, in any case, they know we're here now . . ."

Stabling their horses at the Orting livery, Jessie and Ki walked with their traveling bags to the hotel. Spring twilight, soft purple and dusty rose, now clouded the town, and they almost overlooked the hotel entrance, which was simply a narrow inset door with a sign that read "BEDS."

Inside, they found themselves in a small, tawdry lobby, half papered with magazine illustrations of horses, dogs, and fat chorus girls plastered to the yellow pine walls with flour-and-water paste. There was a short counter with a lamp and a handmade checkerboard on it. Behind the counter, the proprietor, a gaunt, red-nosed man, was playing checkers with an unshaven man who stank of filth and sweat. On the wall behind the proprietor hung a rack of keys; by the end of the counter, rough timber stairs led upward.

It was worse than Abbott had led her to expect, Jessie thought. Still, it was this or nothing, and however bad the bed proved to be, she had slept in worse. "Do you have two rooms for the night? And how much?"

The proprietor dragged a register from beneath the counter. "One night, one dollar. Each. Was you aimin' to be around long? The longer you stay, the cheaper it gits."

"We'll see," Jessie said. She signed the register, and as Ki followed suit, she laid two silver dollars on the counter.

The proprietor took two keys from the rack behind the counter. "Rooms five and six, respectively."

Picking up the keys, Ki looked them over, both sides. "There're no numbers on them. Which is which?"

"Take your fancy. Any key fits any lock."

"Figures," Jessie murmured. "Is there a restaurant nearby?"

The other man spoke up. "Depot Café, two blocks east."

As they started for the door, the proprietor said, "No need to lug them bags along with you. I'll keep 'em for you."

"Thanks just the same," Jessie said, thinking about the keys. "We'll take them along."

The proprietor and the vagrant looked blankly polite.

The Depot Café had a stagecoach schedule propped in its shopfront window. Jessie and Ki both ordered the dinner special—a platter of fried steaks, potatoes hashed up with onion chunks, and biscuits. Ki buttered a couple of extra biscuits, eating them as they headed back to the hotel. He had just finished the second biscuit when they noticed two men blocking the hotel entrance. The pair were hunkered down on their heels in the doorway, waiting silently until Jessie and Ki halted a few feet from them.

Then one of them spoke. "It's her, all right. Like they was saying up around the watering trough. The tall, struttin' sweetie in gent's clothin', sided by a Chink servant. What would you guess she's got in that valise?"

Actually, Ki was carrying a valise; Jessie had a

leather telescope bag. But they had no intention of correcting the speaker, a young man of perhaps nineteen, with a loose, corrupt mouth and an unnatural sheen to his eyes. His clothes were not a poor man's, but the next thing to it. He wore two guns, butts protruding forward cross-draw style.

The man beside him asked, "Are you Miz Starbuck?"

Jessie nodded warily. "Why?"

"Some friends of yours been wantin' us to talk to you," he said, rising. This one was angular, sinewy, dressed in faded brown duck trousers and a quill vest, with his gunbelt and revolver looking mighty well cared for. "Friends that don't want you an' your pard to get mixed up in somethin' that ain't none of your business."

"What friends?" Jessie demanded.

"Folks who sorta worry about your health, I reckon."

"Nice of them," Jessie said levelly. "And who're you?"

"Call me Mac, if'n you hanker. But shucks, names don't mean nothin'. We're just bringin' you a message, to stay outta these parts. Pierce County from Puyallup to Wilkeson is poison meat so far as y'all are concerned."

The two-gun, cross-draw youth said sneeringly, "I'll tell you what I think she's got in that valise. Lace and ribbons and fancy perfume-soap for her fancy man here."

Ki put his valise down. Paying no attention to Mac, he said pleasantly, "What's your name?"

"I ain't got no name," the youth replied, winking at his companion.

"Your family can't make up its mind, eh?" Ki said sociably. "I had a dog like that once. I kept putting it off, and putting it off. And ended by calling him Spunky."

The youth whipped upright with the speed of a rattlesnake. But as quick as he was, Mac was quicker, standing between him and Ki. "Come along," he said, nudging the two-gun kid with his shoulder. "We done delivered our piece."

They ambled across the street and into the nearest saloon.

When they were gone, Ki picked up his valise, turned the china doorknob and held the door open for Jessie to enter the hotel ahead of him.

In the lobby, the proprietor was still playing checkers, but now with himself. When he saw Jessie, he said, "Have a nice visit with your friends, ma'am?"

"Yes," she said.

They stared at each other a moment, each poker-faced.

Ki led the way up the steps and along a greasy-matted corridor, searching the line of doors for their rooms. When Jessie was alone in hers with the lamp lighted, she locked the door and wedged the room's one chair under the knob. There were also a humpbacked bed, a tall wardrobe, a combination bureau and washstand, and a window whose shade she pulled down and secured tightly. She slept that night with her pistol under her blanket by her knee, Texas-emergency style.

Ki, too, slept fitfully, and awoke early when rousted by a passing stagecoach in the street below. He lay listening to the hoofbeats, the rattle of trace chains, the whoa-ing of the driver as the stage clattered to a halt a couple of blocks away; then, out of curiosity, he got up and padded to the window. Outside, a scarlet sun streaked with smoky clouds was just splitting the horizon. By craning his neck, Ki could see the Flaming Geyser stage up by the Depot Café, loading a mailbag, some freight, and three passengers.

One looked to be a drummer, the second a farmer; but it was the third who drew Ki's alert attention—an auburn-haired girl no older than Jessie and probably less, her nubile body covered by a blue brocade dress. She paused for a moment, face tilted toward the sunrise, allowing Ki to glimpse features that were at once delicate and firm: mouth wide and stubborn, a nose angled at a delicate tilt. Then she turned and stepped into the stage. The driver and the guard, testing the lever of his rifle, climbed up on the high seat. The driver's hoarse voice and cracking whip started the team in motion, and Ki watched as the coach rolled heavily on, heading eastward along the route to Wilkeson.

Two hours later, Jessie and Ki were fed, packed, and riding out on the same road. For the rest of the morning they followed the rutted wagon trail, crossing the river valley and carving higher into the hills through a series of canyons, dips, and switchback grades. Along about lunchtime, they reached the section where the trouble on the Flaming Geyser line centered. They would have known that by the wrinkled, worried face of the relay-station agent when they stopped at South Prairie to talk to him, if by nothing else.

South Prairie and the relay station were one and the same—three blocky, midget log cabins crammed into each other, with a squat common chimney of limestone rising up out of the meeting of their roofs, and a pole-fence corral taking up most of the back clearing. A typical road ranch, Jessie and Ki surmised as they approached. One of the side cabins would be a sort of dormitory, with built-in bunks, probably; the cabin at the rear would be the kitchen and living quarters for the agent; the other side cabin, the one with the door, would be the dining room and a kind of guest parlor. It was there, by the hitching rack in front of the door, that they reined in. Dismounting, they noticed signs that the road ranch had fallen into disrepair at one time, but had been painstakingly rejuvenated, repainted—a stomach-churning orange—reroofed with cedar shingles, and decorated with window boxes.

The interior seemed equally inviting, serene and secure. The table, a long trestle thing, had been lye-scrubbed for cleanliness until it was bleached. The floor was so clean that they could've eaten off it, and wouldn't have minded, the food proved to be so good. But as the agent, a spindly looking fellow with round fish eyes and the embarrassing name of Ethel, placed a steaming tureen between Jessie and Ki, he didn't act serene or secure at all.

"Trouble all the time," he said mournfully. "This job used to keep me busy enough, but they wasn't nothin' else to worry about. Now it seems like every owlhooter in the entire Territory is flocking 'tween here and Wilkeson. Just last week we lost a stage outside Zenobia."

"Robbed?" Jessie asked.

"It didn't carry no strongbox, but them gunmen took every watch and dollar the passengers had. Cut the hosses loose and burnt the coach. We had the devil's own time takin' care of them folks and gettin' them on their way again. That coach didn't cost copper cents, either, ma'am."

"How about the driver and guard?" Ki asked. "Were they hurt?"

"Gary Goldfarb, the guard, he got a slug through his shoulder. More like a warnin'. Other'n that, nobody was hurt. The mailsacks were ripped wide open and the letters scattered to the wind. It was a mess!"

"How about other things happening?"

"There's been plenty, ma'am. The week afore that coach got burnt, a freighter was takin' milling equipment to Wilkeson. Masked galoots jumped it and sent the driver on with the team after cuttin' loose the wagon. You'd never guess what they done with that heavy machinery."

"It'd be a big load to carry off," Ki allowed.

"They didn't. They fixed explosives all over that

load and sent 'er sky-high. There wasn't a piece of metal bigger'n my hand when the law got there." Ethel, sighing, ladled soup into their bowls and went on to give a long list of wrecked coaches and wagons, senseless holdups with the bandits touching little of value, simply destroying equipment or stealing mail that contained only ordinary personal and business letters. "Hate to 'fess, but I'm ready to quit. I don't think the line can take many more losses, and callin' the law in don't seem to do no good."

"Is the law honest?" Ki asked.

"As the day is long," the agent vouched. "It ain't Ezra Maxwell's fault. He's posted in Zenobia, the only deputy sheriff for this whole area, and there're just too many things happenin' too fast for one lawman to get anywheres. He follows a trail, it vanishes, and when he comes back there're two more pieces of devilment been done miles apart."

Jessie nodded. "Any idea who the bandits might be?"

"Nary a glimmer. Maxwell's frettin' about so many driftin' this way all at once, like they was all in one big band operatin' powerfully smooth. He'd sure have his hands full fightin' a bunch like them, assumin' he could ever run 'em to ground. It's downright discouragin'."

"Well, you hang in here a while longer. Maybe something can be worked out." *And maybe not,* Jessie thought grimly. She hoped her encouragement wasn't just so much pissing in the wind . . .

Gathering their rested horses from the corral, Jessie and Ki started off again. The South Prairie relay station dropped behind them, and after about five miles, they began skirting the conifer-clad flanks of the Cascades. The road wound increasingly around the low spurs of the mountains, sometimes going through them by way of narrow, rock-strewn passes; often the riders could see only a few yards ahead.

They were approaching a stretch of tall blocky slopes when Ki shifted irritably in his saddle and told Jessie in a low voice, "Something's wrong."

Jessie twisted about, but saw no vestige of life. "Where?"

"In the air, underfoot, damned if I know." He nodded toward the slopes. "That's the highest point around this spot, enough stone to hide an army. Drop behind me, Jessie, and cover my back."

Obeying, Jessie followed Ki's lead when he jiggled the reins gently so that his horse slowed to a walking pace. In line, padding softly, almost noiselessly, they broached the next turn and saw that the rutted dirt road was straight for a distance.

Ahead was the stagecoach Ki had seen leaving Orting that morning.

They had finally caught up with it, but in a sense that wasn't wildly surprising. The coach had stopped dead in the road and the passengers were descending, the men with their hands in the air.

Bandits had caught up with it as well. A group of horsemen with drawn revolvers surrounded the coach, men with hard, stubbled faces who hadn't bothered with masks. Under the harsh orders of their leader, the guard and driver carefully climbed down from the high seat. When they reached the ground, the leader moved his horse out from the group and grinned at the passengers, his loud voice carrying clearly to Jessie and Ki.

"No robbery, folks! We're just borrowin' this coach an' team."

"But how do we get to Wilkeson?" the drummer demanded.

The outlaw laughed. "Mister, that's your problem. You can head for Wilkeson or back to the relay station. There's a little town ahead called Zenobia. You might get some help there."

"This is an outrage!" the traveler stormed. "I'll report this to the law. I'll see you hanged some day!"

The outlaw's laughter abruptly left his lips, his square face turning dark and thunderous. Slowly, deliberately, he dismounted and strode over to the drummer. For a moment he looked the man over, heavy hands on his hips. Then without warning his fist lashed out, the knuckles striking squarely in the man's face. Falling to the ground, the drummer lay too stunned to move, his nose and mouth bleeding. The girl passenger gave one short gasp, then whirled on the outlaw with blazing eyes.

“When he comes around,” the outlaw growled before she could lash out at him, “tell him he’s lucky he ain’t got a bullet hole in him. Tell him . . . hell, I’ll bring him around myself.”

He stepped forward and bent over the drummer. The big fist knotted in the man’s coat and jerked the limp man upward. The outlaw started swinging, his heavy open palm smacking loudly against the man’s cheeks, his brutality goaded on by the hoots and hollers of the other outlaws.

Then, like a crack of a whip, a gunshot echoed among the rocks. The bandit leader staggered, releasing the drummer and clapping his right hand on his left arm, which was suddenly dangling limp and leaking blood. A second shot blasted another robber who had twisted around, revolver blurring up to meet the new challenge. The robber fell out of his saddle and lay silent.

A clear voice shouted, “You’re all covered! Stand hitched!”

Along with his mounted men, the bandit leader stood uncertainly a moment, glaring eyes darting toward the rocks that lined the road. Then Jessie and Ki rode into view, Jessie with her pistol leveled and Ki targeting them with her saddle carbine—though that didn’t squelch the leader from demanding gun action from his gang.

“You got irons! No squinty-eye can see to aim worth crap! An’ no female pistol-packer’s any lady or any shootist!”

"That's what we're afraid of," a robber responded. "Either of 'em might go wavery and hit us by mistake, if they take notion to fire point-blank at you again, boss."

"Will you quit stallin'? You yaller pissants, pull on 'em!"

"Pull, and you'll push daisies," Jessie warned.

One of them, a chinless runt at the far end of the bunched robbers, went berserk in panic and bolted up the road. The next second, another gunman was following his example; the second after that, the rest of the mounted outlaws, with the courage of desperation, were urging their horses into gallops and blasting indiscriminately as they fled.

Opening fire, Jessie and Ki downed three outlaws almost at once. The driver and the guard seized the opportunity, immediately clambering up the coach to retrieve their weapons left on the high seat. The outlaw leader, half-turning to run for his own horse, ignored his wounded arm and whipped up his revolver, firing at Jessie the same instant she shot at him. His bullet went wide. Jessie's truer aim snatched him off his feet, her slug smashing into his stomach. He landed on his rump, his head wobbling as if to deny he was dead.

With yells of fright and pain, the vicious outlaws were intent on tearing for the next bend in the road, with a few lunging off-trail to vanish among the trees and underbrush. Jessie, Ki, the driver, and the guard sent streams of lead hissing and crackling in pursuit. They had the satisfaction of hearing a wild thrashing and howling, but mainly from the dirt-churning distance came the rattle of hooves, the sound fast diminishing. They ceased firing.

The girl passenger had run to the drummer's side and was dabbing ineffectually at his bloodied face with a lacy handkerchief. The driver leaped for the team to quiet them, and the guard went over to thank Jessie for her timely intervention. Ki went about checking the dead outlaws. Intent on his task, he slowly went through their pockets one by one, laid articles on the dirt beside him, studied them, and carefully replaced them. Muslin tobacco sack and brown cigarette papers; a bottle opener; a lucky rabbit's foot that had been carried until the fur had worn off, leaving it pretty odd-looking; fourteen dollars and nine cents; a small striped paper sack with some horehound candy; and a walnut shell with a tiny glass window. Ki held the shell to the sunlight; inside was an intimate boudoir scene. That, apparently, was the lot. Like the ambushers yesterday, the bandits traveled anonymously, and light.

"Guess we oughta stack the bodies over on the shoulder," the driver said when Ki was done. "When we stop at Zenobia, we'll report the holdup to Deputy Maxwell and let him figure their buryin'. You're accompanying us there, ain't you, Miz Starbuck?"

Jessie nodded. "Zenobia's our destination."

"Well, I can't say I mind y'all remainin' with us at least that far. There's nothing to prevent more trouble later on, but holdup men will likely think twice before jumpin' two well-armed riders, as well as me and Ralph."

Jessie reckoned that made sense, and looked at Ki to see if he agreed. He was looking at the girl. And the girl was looking right back, with eyes darker than her auburn hair, provocative and challenging. *Good grief,* Jessie thought. *If there's a young female in heat within fifty miles, he somehow gets to her.*

Chapter 3

The depot in Zenobia was not nearly as large as that at Orting. Still, there was a general room and a private office for the local agent; and out in back were stables, a corral, and a smithy shed. Across the road, facing the station, was a line of weathered, ramshackle shops and offices, a couple of restaurants, a laundry, and three saloons that Jessie could count. The street, she guessed, would be called Main or Front. There were smaller lanes cutting into it, and diagonally across it, about twenty feet up a side lane bordering one of the saloons, she could glimpse a sign sticking out from a building lighted by a lantern on an iron hook. The sign said ROOMS, and was decorated by a painted horseshoe and a four-leaf clover. The street was livening up with the approach of evening, early night-bloomers cropping up among the plain folk doing business and workers knocking off for the day. All in all, Zenobia struck her as quite an active little lumbertown.

At the moment, most of the activity was centered around the stagecoach parked in front of the depot. News of the attempted holdup had traveled fast, and within minutes of the coach arriving, townsfolk and bar patrons were grouping around, asking dumb questions and giving dumber opinions.

In the thick of it, trying to be heard above the blather, stood Deputy Sheriff Maxwell, a knotty, middle-aged man with a sad, drooping mouth and baby blue eyes. Evidently he'd shaved that morning, but in a rush: his face was mottled with patches of brassy stubble that the razor had missed. Now, having interviewed the driver, guard, passengers, Jessie, and Ki, he was dealing with the irate Flaming Geyser agent. The agent—whose name, Jessie gathered from the conversation, was Sherwin Lysander—was a stocky gent in a dowdy, dark brown twill suit and a beige suede vest.

With a gravelly voice and permanently inflated cheeks that always looked as though they were on the verge of whistling secretly and mysteriously—and sometimes did—Lysander faced the sheriff with fists on hips and pompously demanded, "And just what are you going to do about it?"

"When you come right down to it," Maxwell said wearily, "I'm afraid the answer is just about nothing."

"Nothing?"

"Don't you see, Lysander? Everything seems to be fixed these days so it comes out nothing." When the agent started to speak, Maxwell interrupted him. "Oh, I'll mount a posse, and we'll ride out there to collect the bodies and look for tracks. Might even be able to trail them a ways. But you know what'll happen? I'll lose 'em like I have before, somewheres up in the rockbeds 'tween the road and White River. That's one of the cussedest sections around."

"It's a stretch, I'll grant you. But I hazard they could drive a buffalo across a snowbank and leave you behind."

"Now, see here, Lysander, you've no call to—"

The sheriff's defense was cut short by a buckskin-clad man sprinting out from the lane on the far side of the depot building. Head bent, he lunged around the corner and tore for the crowd, apparently not seeing the sheriff but figuring there was safety in numbers. And in pursuit pounded a group of yelling brutes—muscular lumberjacks, by the look of their plaid mackinaws, stagged wool pants, and caulked boots. Even as the crowd stared, the buckskinner, who was perhaps a score of paces distant, stumbled, and sprawled headlong in the street. A big bruiser, with a jaw like a hunk of pickled beef, came upon the fallen man, whipped out a revolver, and slashed viciously.

The man on the ground cried out as the barrel ripped a gash in his forehead. He writhed under the blow, tried to rise, and fell back, groaning. The revolver raised to slap his face with steel again.

Instead, Ki intervened. Actually, he had started

to intervene the instant he assessed the situation, but it took him time to shove through the bystanders and get to the fallen man. Only a moment, perhaps, but time enough for the first, and last, of the pistol-whipping. Then it was Ki's moment to sweep in and strike. He launched at the big jack, his left hand gripping the man in a hold that made him drop his revolver. The callused heel of his right hand chopped the jack between his eyes—not enough to kill him, but enough to make him damn well wish he were dead.

As the jack collapsed alongside his pistol-whipped victim, a second jack thrust forward, cursing and centering his revolver. But already Ki was knuckle-punching the new jack in the throat, tempering his blow so as not to break the neck, but forcefully enough to hurt like blazes. This jack choked, hawked, and gagged, tears of pain springing into his eyes. Ki followed through by kicking him in the side of the knee, collapsing one side, then caught his right arm, crunched down on it with an elbow, and brought his own knee into the jack's hip. The jack dropped, stunned.

"Cut it out!" Maxwell shouted, pushing to the fore.

"Hell I will! Take this!"

This was the telltale click of a hammer. Ki had already seen the third jack slide the weapon out of a coat pocket; he had been keeping track of it peripherally until ready to deal with it. Now, stepping over the second jack, Ki caught hold of the third one's right arm and left shoulder with his hands. With the gunhand locked useless, Ki moved his right foot slightly in back of the jack, so that as the jack began tumbling sideways, Ki was able to dip to his right knee and yank viciously. His elbow-drop worked perfectly; the jack sailed upside down and collapsed jarringly on top of the second jack, flattening them both to the street.

"Now, cut it out!" Maxwell bellowed again.

This time the jacks obeyed, the three on the ground struggling upright, wincing and cussing, while the others congregated around with mouths agape. The beef-jawed bruiser sat on his haunches, rubbing his right wrist and glaring stonily at Ki.

"What the devil's the notion?" he demanded.

"And what's the notion of taking a whack at a jigger who's down and can't help himself?" Ki countered.

"He was warned to stay outta this town!"

"What is he—a pickpocket, horse thief?"

"Worse! He's a trapper!"

"Never heard tell of any law against being a trapper," Ki replied, glancing first at the buckskinned trapper, who'd remained where he was in the street, evidently well-satisfied to be forgotten for the moment. Then Ki glanced at Sheriff Maxwell, whose features looked chiseled in grim stone. "Never heard it was against the law for trappers to come into a town."

"It ain't, not in Zenobia, leastwise," Maxwell answered in a voice that could've etched crystal. Then he addressed the big man. "Bender, I've told you about ruckus-raisin' in town. If that fellow on the ground puts a charge against you, I'll lock up the whole passel of you."

Straightening, the bruiser named Bender shrugged. "You couldn't make the charge stick, Maxwell. This is log country."

"I know it is. But there's a limit, and clobberin' folks is going beyond it, even if they do happen to be trappers."

"Who clobbered who? If there's law-doggin' to do around here, go lock *him* up"—Bender pointed to Ki—"for clobberin' of us. Mighty nigh twisted my arm outta the socket!"

"Reckon you had it comin'," the sheriff growled. "Okay, Bender, you and your crew trail out of here and head back for your camp. You've raised enough hell for today."

Bender snarled something under his breath, but nevertheless, he turned and stalked back toward the lane, his followers trooping after him. "Mister, I'll be seein' you!" he flung over his shoulder at Ki.

"Look close the first time," Ki responded coolly, " 'cause you might not get a second look."

Bender spat an oath and kept on walking. When he'd vanished with his crewmen around the corner and into the side lane, Sheriff Maxwell turned his attention to the trapper still prostrate on the ground. "Why can't you hellions keep out down hereabouts? Do your buyin' at the tradin' posts."

The trapper got painfully to his feet. He was a little old man with a leathery face and grizzled hair and beard. His eyes were a milky blue, but steady enough. "It's a far piece between posts, Sheriff, and we can't go navigatin' them pack trails every time we need some sugar and beans. If the posts *had* sugar and beans, which half the time they don't. And when they do, Fitzpatrick and Locke are chargin' thievery prices. A hundred dollars for a barrel of potatoes."

"A hund—!" Maxwell was aghast.

"Yep, an' twenty-five for a bag of flour." The trapper shot Maxwell an accusing look. "Fitzpatrick and Locke, they blame their gougin' on account of all the freighter holdups recently. They claim that once the owlhooters are caught—*if* they're ever caught—then they can afford to lower their—"

"Slit my gizzard, I'll nab 'em!" the sheriff vowed hastily. "And I hafta admit, it's a free country for you. But there's some doubt about you fellers being 'specially law-abidin'. Where's your horse?"

"Got a wagon around back there," the trapper said, thumbing toward the general store. "A bunch of us chipped in for supplies."

"Okay, load up what you came for, and get back to your patch before something else happens."

The trapper nodded, and turned to Ki. "Thanks, son. I reckon you saved me a prime hiding. But I'm afeared you made a bad enemy by doin' it. Bender Busch is tarnation mean."

"I've a hunch his bark is worse than his bite," Ki replied affably.

"You're wrong," Maxwell said, as the elderly trapper shuffled off toward the general store. "And as for you, well, we don't need rowdies who take the law into their own hands."

"You appear to be well supplied with that kind, all right."

Seeing that Ki's remark was not improving the sheriff's temper, Jessie quickly spoke up. "Is there a livery here? And where would you recommend we eat and stay the night?"

"The stable's across the street an' down a block," Maxwell answered. "Only place to stay over is the Neskowin, but they got a dining room that puts out good food." Then, eyeing the cluster of bystanders, he declared, "I'm gatherin' a posse, and you're volunteerin' to join. Who knows, maybe we'll backtrack them heisters this time. They've had all the breaks so far, but they're due for a slip-up or for their luck to run out."

"Well, I ain't holdin' my breath," Lysander said, turning to his driver and guard. "Soon's your passengers have et their evenin' meal, get a fresh team hitched up and move on out. You're running late as it is."

The crowd rapidly went their separate ways—the driver, guard, and three passengers angling for the closer of the two restaurants, while Maxwell and the locals he'd volunteered for posse duty hustled for their horses. Since most of the horses were stabled at the livery, Jessie and Ki decided to hold off going there until the crush was gone. A fortunate decision, for while waiting, they chanced to overhear a conversation between Agent Lysander and a mid-elderly, competent-looking timberman, who resembled a sedate schoolmaster more than a tough-as-nails manager of a logging operation. But it became obvious that he was a manager or superintendent or some such high honcho when Lysander gave a start at sight of him, then said effusively, "Why, hello there, Mr. Marmont. I didn't see you amongst the crowd. How long's it been since you come to—"

"Lysander," Marmont cut in tersely, "is the westbound stage going out as usual at week's end, or ain't it?"

Lysander looked astonished. "Sure, it's going out as usual!"

"Then why'd you say it was leaving a day earlier, for the time being?"

"I never said no such thing!"

"Y'mean, you didn't send word up to the Yamhill Camp?"

"Of course, I didn't! Who told you I sent such word?"

"A man on horseback," Marmont said. "Never seen him before. Came by last night, told me you'd told him to be sure to tell me about the change in schedule."

"All this tellin' is giving me a headache," Lysander complained. "Well, I'm telling you now I never told nobody no such thing. I'd like to know who pulled that trick. Musta thought he was pretty smart."

Marmont frowned, worried. "I swore I'd never let a cash shipment lay overnight anywhere between here and Orting. Why, your station alone has been robbed twice already."

Lysander raised a protesting hand. "Don't need to worry any more about that. I got me a good, strong safe now, that nothing short o' stump-blasting powder can open. You headin' downcountry, Mr. Marmont?"

"No, I'm on my way over to the Soda Peak camp. Now, listen, Lysander. By week's end, there'll be a wad of cash here, set to go out to pay for new equipment. See that you take care of it."

"You can rest easy on that score," the agent assured him, and grinned confidently as Marmont grunted good-bye and turned away. Instantly, the grin died, and Lysander stomped into the depot, slamming the door.

Soon the sheriff and his posse stormed out of town, passing Jessie and Ki as they headed for the livery stable. Jessie gazed absently at the riders, then glanced thoughtfully back at the depot while mulling over the conversation she'd heard.

"Ki," she said at last, "did you catch any sign at all that Lysander was expecting us or knew who we are?"

"No, none. Of course, he could've been acting."

"Perhaps. But I didn't catch any hint, either, so I have to figure that he isn't party to whoever rigged the ambush yesterday. On the other hand, he certainly was flustered when he first saw Marmont. *Did* he send word up to the logging camp?"

"If Lysander did, it's because he wanted the money brought here for safekeeping the day before it normally would've arrived. Why?"

"Offhand, I can't figure a reason, unless—and it's a blame big unless—he planned on lifting it, or having it lifted." Jessie shook her head. "Still, I can't help wondering if that agent is up to something . . ."

★

Chapter 4

Checking around town, questioning lumberjacks, shopkeepers, and others, Jessie and Ki gleaned bits of knowledge that failed to add up to a respectable whole, much less answer her concerns. It seemed clear that the plundering of the freight and stage line was a systematized business, no doubt the work of a ring of thieves. They pilfered not only every kind of portable goods, but also stock: three valuable stage teams had been stolen.

"No wonder that broker, that Horace Mahoney, wouldn't meet the old terms," Ki remarked at one point. "I'm surprised he and the Northern Pacific didn't back out of the deal altogether."

Jessie agreed. "Abbott's been in tight places, but never before has he tried keeping his feet on so slippery an edge."

The row between timbermen and trappers was one they had run into a time or two before.

The trappers, for the most part mountainmen squeezed by advancing civilization to smaller and smaller hunting grounds, considered the timbermen as interlopers and land-ravagers, even though the timbermen may have bought their vast forested tracts. To a trapper, all wilderness was open country, open year 'round, despite his not holding any real title to it. To a timberman, trappers were trespassers and nuisances and a danger to logging operations, what with their concealed steel traps and the like. As a result, there were the makings for a nice steamy kettle of devil's brew.

This feud, which had boiled over once already that day, erupted again later that evening, while Jessie and Ki were eating dinner. They had gone to the Neskowin and, after signing in, had stowed their bags in rooms like those of just about any other smalltown hotel: unpretentious, moderately clean, and, despite windows propped open with sticks of kindling, somehow stuffy.

They found the Spartan dining room off the lobby, its only decor other than the tables and chairs a poorly mounted elk head. Although an inner wall and door separated the lobby from the dining room, there was no partition at all between the dining room and the saloon; the two, in fact, were one large room divided only by their furnishings. Where the dining-room furnishings ended, they were replaced by smaller round tables and different chairs, and a scarred oakplank bar running the length of the side wall. There was a sprinkling of customers in both parts, some wolfing down food, others bellying up to the bar or haggling over cards at the tables, most clad in the flannel shirts, cord pants, and laced boots common to timberland life. None appeared to be the kind you'd hanker to invite to a tea party.

Except, perhaps, for one individual. This one Ki noticed while he and Jessie were giving their dinner orders to a stubby, rheumy-eyed waiter.

"Roast beef, fried potatoes, canned pears, and coffee," Jessie was saying when Ki nudged her.

"The girl," he said. "Gwendolyn."

Shifting, Jessie cast a glance where Ki was indicating. "My, my, gotten to exchange names with her, have you?"

"I overheard her when she gave her name to the sheriff," Ki said, smiling across to where the girl was seated. "I see she didn't leave with the other two passengers when the stage pulled out."

"Amazing deduction."

"Maybe she's staying over here, too."

"Or maybe she's waiting to be met by her three-hundred-pound fiancé who has a jealous streak, a mean temper, and a double-bladed axe." Her caustic comment did not faze Ki, Jessie saw. He kept on giving the girl his best grin, Gwendolyn flashing her teeth in return, eyelashes aflutter, bosom aheaving, radiating a sort of vixenish appeal guaranteed to addle male wits.

Presently, the waiter returned with their food. As he was serving, a raucous laugh burst from the barroom, drawing their attention. A fat man with muttonchops had risen from a poker table and was turning toward the bar. "Pour a round for all them idiot cardsharps there," he crowed loudly. "It's on me, but they been paying for it."

"Hugh Fitzpatrick, co-owner of some trading posts," the waiter remarked. "He's liable to hooraw when he wins good. Can't fault him. His wins are few and far between."

They eyed the man with keener interest. Fitzpatrick had his hair parted in the middle, and cherubic eyes twinkled deep in the pink rolls of fat forming his cheeks. His trousers and unbuttoned suit jacket had to have been custom tailored to fit his expansive girth, and his buttoned vest and shirt looked fit to bursting, yet he moved to the bar with a lightness of foot at variance with his bulk.

The lumberjacks lining the bar shifted to allow Fitzpatrick entry, casting him hostile glances, which he ignored. One hulking jack with a truculent eye and a bad-tempered face, however, kept shooting the trading-post owner savage glares. Finally, downing his whiskey, the jack started along the bar toward Fitzpatrick.

The waiter gulped, almost dropping his tray. "Uh-oh."

"So!" the jack barked in a drink-slurred voice that carried throughout the room. "So you got cash to gamble, eh? You're still raking in money from them trappers?"

Fitzpatrick turned slowly and smiled at the jack. "Reckon that's right. Their money's good as anybody else's. I'm in business to do business."

"And if you keep on doin' it, you ain't gonna be around long! You'll end up findin' yourself on the end of a rope, if they can find a rope strong enough to haul all the tallow you pack."

"Sure, sure. Reckon it'd take a strong rope—and a strong man to handle it. You figure to be strong enough?"

Fitzpatrick asked pleasantly enough, but his intimation was clear. The big jack flushed darkly; his eyes gleamed; his thick calloused hands opened and shut. He took a quick step toward Fitzpatrick, squaring his shoulders belligerently.

Things happened, and happened fast. A dimpled hand shot out and gripped the jack by the slack of his shirt front, raised him clean off his feet, and slammed him to the floor with bone-breaking force. Fitzpatrick smiled down amiably at the prostrate jack, and for a moment the jack just lay there, dazed.

Then, with a roar of rage, the jack bounded to his feet, clawing for a revolver in his jacket pocket. He never got it out. The same pudgy hand that had floored him moved like a flicker of a hawk's wing to Fitzpatrick's left armpit. The jack stiffened as he stared into a stubby, three-barreled "over and under" .32 derringer. Fitzpatrick's pleasant voice broke the tense silence.

"About six feet and three inches will give plenty of headroom."

The jack "got" the peculiar remark. His face blanched, his hand dropping away from his pocket. Fitzpatrick continued to smile, his strangely thin lips in contrast to his plump cheeks. His eyes were like bits of polished flint, with all the twinkle gone from them.

"Fitzpatrick hires out for undertakerin', along with running his tradin' posts," the waiter explained in a breathless whisper. "He's measurin' the gent for a coffin."

For a long moment, the tableau held. Then the jack slowly turned and shambled for the saloon entrance that fronted the main street. The breath men were holding was exhaled in gusty sighs that filled the room with sound. Fitzpatrick deftly slid his gun back into its shoulder holster and smilingly raised a brimming glass—which the bartender had hastily provided—with a plump hand that did not spill a drop.

The room hummed with conversation, but soon interest in the drinks and games lessened the excitement. The girl Gwendolyn finished her dinner, and with a perky twitch of her rump, sashayed out through the lobby door. While Ki was eyeing her, Jessie continued to study the smiling trading-post owner, who returned to the poker table sipping another drink, apparently forgetting all about the gun incident.

"Hugh Fitzpatrick seems like quite a fellow," Jessie remarked when the waiter brought coffee and cherry pie. "Quite strong and quick on his feet for someone his size."

"Yeah, he shore is," the waiter responded. "Sits a horse well, too, though it takes a mighty stout one to pack him. He's got a shrewd business head, to boot. Came in a while ago and bought into a chain of posts owned by Urias Locke, who never could do much with 'em. But Fitzpatrick makes a profit; he makes sure of that. He's had several run-ins with the trappers he cheats, and with the loggers who don't like him sellin' to trappers, but he 'lows as he's got a right to sell to anyone who's got money to buy with. Reckon he has."

Smiling lightly, Jessie proffered no comment, but left the gabby waiter a sizable tip when paying the bill.

Shortly afterward, she and Ki retired for the night. Her room, across from Ki's, was near the head of the second-floor corridor. Locking the door, she removed her boots and holstered shellbelt, loosened her jeans, stuck her pistol under the pillow, and climbed under the covers thinking she would go right out. But like the night before, sleep proved elusive. Her mind was too distressed by the events, too disturbed by the feuding and banditry igniting the area, to let her relax. She lay pondering in the dark, hearing a subdued murmur of night activity from the main street before finally dozing off . . .

Some time after midnight Jessie snapped wide awake. She didn't move for a moment, eyes circling the dark room, hand feeling for the heavy gun under her pillow. Then she realized what had awakened her—faint shouts, growing louder, coming from the street. Quietly, she rose from her bed and walked to the window, seeing figures running, then glimpsing an angry red glow above the roofline.

"Fire!" she heard shouted. "It's sure a-goin', too!"

Jessie hastily dressed and buckled on her gunbelt. In the hallway, she met Ki, who was just emerging from his room, and together they hurried down to the lobby. The night clerk was by the hotel entry, gesturing excitedly.

"Big fire! The stage depot is burnin' fast!"

"More trouble for poor old Abbott," Jessie groaned as they brushed past the clerk. "And not a thing we could've done to stop it!"

Out in the street, they joined others who were heading for the depot. The blaze was radiating like a fiery beacon, its smoky torch distorting the night sky, moonlight filtering through it eerie and unreal. They saw that the fire was so far confined to the structures in back of the streetside office and waiting room. Bucket brigades had already formed, and were concentrating for the most part on the the barn containing grain and feed, which was a roaring furnace. Those not in a brigade were trying to save equipment stored in another portion of the rear yard, and still others rushed for the stables. The loud, frightened whinnying of frantic animals sounded above the crackling roar of the flames.

Jessie and Ki joined the desperate, determined throng by the stable door. Among them were Sheriff Maxwell, wearing boots and a pair of red longjohns; and the agent, Sherwin Lysander, with only pants and shoes on, his face haggard.

"A dozen horses in there!" he exclaimed, at Jessie's swift query. "We have to get them out!"

"How'd the fire start?"

"How'n hell would I know? I was home, asleep!"

Choking smoke rolled from the cracks and vents and the door of the stable, although the fire had not as yet turned into an inferno. Ki, standing poised while Jessie was questioning Lysander, now plunged inside the stable. Smoke blinded him, but he felt his way back to the farthest stall. A horse there was making frenzied efforts to escape, but Ki's soothing voice seemed to calm the animal. Inside the stall, he felt the horse tremble, but when he tried to lead the animal out, it would not leave. Ki was fully aware of his own danger, but here was something he could do, so he wasted no time. Ripping off his shirt, he tied it over the animal's head. Grasping the halter, he led the horse out into the passage and then to safety in the wide yard. Willing hands took the animal.

The glow from the burning feed barn grew brighter and the yard was brilliantly lighted as Ki again headed for the stable door. A handful of other brave souls began following him inside. Jessie was about to join, when abruptly she heard a vicious whine close to her head and whirled instantly, hand slashing down to her gun. But nobody near had a weapon in hand. Another bullet sped close by, the report of the weapon drowned out by the crackle and roar of the fire. A cloud of smoke descended into the yard; for a moment, she was hidden from the mysterious ambusher. When the smoke lifted, Jessie was deep in the excited crowd, working her way toward the front of the yard.

Moving swiftly, hidden by the crowd, she reached a vantage point by the wide gate. The lift of flames brought the roofs out clearly, and her keen eyes scanned them. At first, she saw nothing and began to wonder if the shots had been fired from the depot roof, as she had first surmised. Then a head slowly raised above the parapet, and a stubble-cheeked man searched the milling crowd before the stable doors. More horses were being led out, and the man on the roof raised himself for a better look.

Darting through the gate into the street, Jessie ran swiftly to the far corner of the depot, then cut into the deep shadows between it and the next building. The walls were smooth and high and she wondered how the ambusher had climbed up to his perch. Then, at the far end, she came upon a barrel set against a log fence. With an agile leap she was on the barrel, arms upstretched to the top of the fence. Fingers clawing for a hold, she boosted herself atop the wall; when she straightened, balancing carefully, she found the edge of the roof within easy reach. Climbing up over the edge of the parapet, she dropped, crouching, to the roof. There was not much cover here, for the red glow of the fire revealed the whole expanse of the roof. At the far edge, she saw the ambusher peering down into the yard below, his rifle held ready for instant use.

Jessie catfooted forward, trusting the man would not hear her above the crackle of the flames and the roars of the crowd below. But some feral instinct made him swivel his head. His startled, muddy eyes staring into her adamant face, the man crouched as if paralyzed, still gripping his rifle. That passed in a split second, however; with a strangled oath, he brought the rifle up, finger slipping with practiced ease to the trigger. Jessie threw herself to one side, fisting her pistol. The rifle cracked spitefully, the bullet whipping past her ear. Before the man could work the lever, Jessie's pistol blasted once and spat death into his face. The man crumpled back against the parapet, his rifle clattering to the roof.

Pistol held ready, Jessie stepped forward to check the man. He was dead, all right, and a total stranger to her. Holstering her pistol, she straightened and looked down into the yard. The bucket brigades had pretty much given up on the barn, which was a raging furnace beyond salvaging, and were dousing adjacent sheds and the stable. Daring flame and smoke, the men were gradually bringing those fires under control, while a handful of others continued darting in and out of the stable doorway. And as she looked, Ki emerged from the stable with the last horse.

Then, again, her gaze focused on the body at her feet, her eyes ice-cold. Someone had engineered a double play here. Had the fire gone unchecked, the loss would have been enormous. Jessie knew what a severe—if not crippling—blow that would have been to Quinn Abbott, but what touched her more personally was that the boss behind the arson had also placed an ambusher here in case she or Ki should happen to get in the line of the rifle sights.

Dragging the dead man across the roof, she unceremoniously dumped him over the side. Then she lowered herself to the top of the fence and down to the ground. Letting the body lie where it had landed, she threaded the narrow passage to the street and back into the depot yard.

For more than an hour longer, the bucket brigades fought the flames. Jessie worked with them, keeping a sharp eye out meanwhile for any further attempts on her life. There just might be, she suspicioned, if that ambusher's body was found by anyone who was in cahoots with him and realized he'd failed. At last the fire died down against the onslaught of the fighters, smoked and smoldered, and finally went out altogether.

A tired, blackened group gathered in the waiting room of the depot. Agent Lysander's pants had a dozen or more holes where embers had struck. Sheriff Maxwell's smile flashed out from an ash-begrimed face. Sweat on Ki's broad, muscular shoulders gleamed in the lamplight.

"How much of a loss, Sherwin?" Maxwell asked.

The agent shrugged wearily. "I estimate a couple of thousand or more. All the hay and feed is gone, and it'll have to be replaced. There's damage to the stable, and the barn'll have to be rebuilt complete."

"Still," Jessie allowed, "everything could have burned."

"Damn—sorry, ma'am—darn near did," Lysander agreed, then grimaced angrily. "That fire was set deliberate! It couldn't have been an accident! Sheriff, you lost the backtrail of those crooks who tried heistin' the stage t'day, but d'you think you might be able to run down the bast—er, bums who torched my yard?"

"Might, might not ever," Maxwell said apologetically. "But I'll do my best."

This, Jessie decided, might or might not be an incompetent lawman, but she was certain he was honest, conscientious, and hardworking.

Indeed, while she and Ki were returning to the hotel, she had a feeling that when Sheriff Maxwell said, "I'll do my best," that was exactly what he meant.

Back in her room, she sat on the edge of the bed and, sighing, pulled off her boots. The floor was cold to her feet as she stripped naked, filled the chipped washbowl with water from the matching pitcher, and used a hand towel to scrub herself. She would have adored a hot bath and a chance to wash her hair, but that would have to be postponed. Constantly rinsing out the towel, she made do by sluicing off the traces of the fire that were clinging like a patina to her face, limbs, breasts, and loins. Briskly she dried herself with the larger, if equally threadbare, bath towel. Her nude flesh tingled, her skin glowing a healthy pink, as she slipped on a clean blouse and jeans she took from her bellows bag. Then, after brushing out her hair and braiding it, she doused the lamp and climbed into bed again.

And lay there like before, thinking. It appeared at this point that finding the arsonist and exposing the power who'd hired him would be nigh impossible. What a mess. Sometimes things worked out simply, and other times they didn't; this was turning out to be one of those times when things didn't, with a vengeance. On that note, Jessie, exhausted, fell into a deep slumber . . .

Ki, too, had decided on a quick cat-bath before retiring. He peeled off his soiled duds and pulled a fresh set from his valise, stacking the fresh set neatly on the bureau for the next day's wearing. He was as unconcerned as Jessie about padding around naked in a strange bedroom—less so, in fact, for he planned to sleep in the buff. He saw no reason to dress in a nightshirt, since he wasn't expecting to go anywhere except to bed.

Washing off the soot and ash, he was working with the towel when he heard someone stop out in the hall, and knuckles tapped on his door.

"Hello? Ki? Are you there?"

Ki recognized Gwendolyn's whispered voice, but he didn't answer at once. Instinctively, his eyes checked the door and the window across from it. The lock was engaged, and the drapes were completely drawn. If he were wise, he'd keep it this way. In a small room, the only trap deadlier than a cross-fire ambush was a compromising situation.

"Ki? I'm all alone. Please let me in."

Ki padded to the door. "What do you want?" he whispered.

"Hurry," Gwendolyn pleaded. "I can't be seen here like this."

The worst, Ki figured; an equivocal answer, dodging the question. But Gwendolyn had him skunked. If she couldn't "be seen here like this," then she definitely couldn't be seen like this banging on his door, begging entry. "Don't come in till I tell you to," he said.

He unlatched the door and went to the bureau, where he took his clean pair of jeans and slipped them on for modesty. Then he called out, and the door widened just enough for Gwendolyn to ease through, sweeping the hem of her floor-length peignoir gown with her as she shut the door behind her—then locking it without being told.

He scratched his bare chest. "I wasn't expecting any visitors, especially ladies."

"Heavens, a girl doesn't grow up in the woods without seeing men in all states of undress," Gwendolyn said, smiling reassuringly as she stepped closer. "And if anyone ought to be thinking improper, it's you of me, coming here alone while everyone else is asleep."

"Such a notion never crossed my mind, Gwendolyn."

"Gwen . . ."

They gravitated toward the bed and sat down, Gwen primly smoothing out the folds of her long, pink-striped nightgown. Her feet were bare, her hair was freshly combed, and she had doused herself with some pleasing, if overpowering, perfume.

"I hope nobody finds me here," she said. She inched closer, her eyes wondrously wide. "Oh, it'd be worse than me in the hall, Ki. I'm always being lectured about not getting too familiar, for fear something might happen."

Ki grinned. "What kind of something?"

"Oh . . . you know. The loggers around all the time, and visitors passing through. My stepdaddy Abe—he owns the sawmill in Wilkeson—he gets powerful mad if I stop and talk much to any of those strangers."

"And you never do?"

"I am now, ain't I?"

"Yeah, you are now . . . and now what?"

"Now what?" She lifted her brows when she repeated Ki's question, and looked sideways at him as she eased still nearer. Ki was pretty fairly convinced by now that her peignoir and perfume were all she had on—except for what she might have had on her mind. "Now what? Why, Ki, now we go to bed."

Ki regarded the short, narrow bed. "Why, Gwen," he said in mock surprise, "are you suggesting we sleep together?"

"Is that so awful?" she murmured, scrutinizing him with her luminous eyes. Her chin was raised and her uptilted face was yearning. "Those frightful outlaws, holding up the stage like they did! Why, you saved me from death, or worse than death. And I'm grateful, very grateful."

Ki was growing interested, but he was also growing worried about playing her game. He wondered how far she'd tease, how far was *too* far; he didn't care to face any more ruckus tonight. "Gwen, you don't have to—"

"I know." She laid her hands on his chest, palms flat, fingers kneading. "I want to." She pressed her body against him then, her arm circling his back and clinging as she kissed him for a long, burning moment. Ki responded with enthusiasm, feeling her lips clinging hungrily, her breasts mashing against his chest, one hand shifting to rub along his thigh, then sliding to his waistband. He was hard as a rock already. He was not wearing his belt, so she had no trouble popping the top button. She lifted her mouth from his, her eyes heavy-lidded and sparkling while she unbuttoned his fly. Raising his hips, Ki let her tug his jeans down, and shuddered reflexively when she then used both hands to grasp his erection. "Ahh, a tree of great standing . . ."

Ki rubbed a hand over her buttocks. "Your nightgown . . ."

"In a minute." She bent over him. As her head lowered, her eyes closed and her full-lipped mouth opened, her pink tongue flicking out to lick his shaft. She seemed to taste him, to see if she liked it; then she fitted her mouth over the satin-smooth crown.

Ki gasped and watched, his eyes flaring when her tongue went into action. His hips began to move slowly, but she stopped and lifted her head. She smiled. Standing up before him, she untied the drawstring of her peignoir and eased the filmy gown down over her breasts and belly. "You, too," she said, letting the nighty drop to puddle around her feet.

Ki pushed his jeans the rest of the way down his legs, and off. Gwen crawled alongside him on the bed, and they spread out lengthwise together, kissing again, their mouths joining moistly. Ki's hand slid into the hollow of her loins, his fingers exploring the lightly haired pad of her mound, then moving lower, inside the lips of her cleft, one finger dipping easily into tight, slippery heat. Her inner muscles working in a rhythmic, squeezing pulse around his finger, she murmured in a low, passionate voice, "Take me. Take me, fill me . . ."

But Ki was not ready to take her. He dallied first, licking the curve of her neck and the tiny lobes of her ears, then lower, nuzzling and kissing one full breast at a time. His groin pressed against her pubic bone, and he began pumping his jutting erection along the sensitive crevice between her thighs, yet never quite penetrating her.

Gwen opened and closed her eyes, gasping and whimpering. Her buttocks jerked and quivered, squirming until her legs were splayed out on the sheets, one of her feet pushing up against the iron frame of the bed. "Don't tease me, Ki," she mewled, panting harshly. "Put it in; oh, please put it in." In a frenzy, she reached between them and placed his taunting manhood against the opening of her moist sheath, prodding Ki into herself with her own trembling fingers.

"Now," she sighed breathlessly, seeming to swallow the whole of him up inside her small belly as she arched her back off the small bed. "Now . . ."

Crooning, Gwen locked her arms and legs firmly around Ki's impaling body. He felt her eager young muscles tightening smoothly around him in a pressuring action of their own, and he set his mind to the delicious ecstasy of the moment. Tighter she wrapped her limbs, deeper she sank her fingernails, rhythmically matching Ki's building tempo as his body pounded hers against the thin mattress.

A squeaky, rickety, bunk-sized bed was not the ideal spot, Ki thought dizzily, for such frantic sport. But that was about all he thought, as they panted in concentration, pummeling each other with ever-quickening strokes. He pumped into her until she was a hot river, until he could feel her not knowing or caring who was inside her, just driving up and down inside her with lavish fanaticism.

"Come with me!" she pleaded loudly, as he felt her inner sheath contracting spasmodically from her erupting orgasm.—Ki climaxed with her, spurting deep inside her belly. And long after they were both good for nothing, Gwen was still wailing, "Come with me; come!"

"Enough," Ki said. "Whoever's in the adjoining rooms will think I'm beating you."

Gwen calmed down and snuggled against him, damp with sweat, her fingers entwining with his. "Yes, yes, I suppose. But Ki, oh, how I wish . . ."

"Wish what?"

"There's a madness going on in these hills, a madness that's taken lives and today threatened to take mine, too. I wish I could stop the madness, but I can't. I must do what I can, make the best of the life I have here . . ." Sighing, she fell asleep.

Ki lay awake beside her, meditating for a time afterward.

Chapter 5

Sometime before dawn, Gwen slipped out of his room. Ki was not sure when; he was just dimly aware of shifting weight as she rose from the bed, and the faint rustlings of her peignoir as she put it on and tiptoed to the door. He slept on soundly, as did Jessie across the hall, until the noise of the morning's activities in the street awakened them.

Dressed, they met in the lobby and saw that the dining room was closed for breakfast. The nearer of the two other restaurants was kitty-corner to the depot, which gave them the opportunity to walk down that way and check the effects of the fire in daylight. Agent Lysander was already there, and showing the marks of strain. He was directing the salvaging of the barn, but there was pitifully little to be saved. In the rosy morning light, the blackened embers stood out like the ugly bones of a skeleton. The whole rear end and most of the roof of the stable would have to be rebuilt.

"And a passel of my horses will have to be replaced, too," Lysander complained. "Some of the ones we saved from the fire bolted before we could corral 'em, so spooked that they're probably in the next county by now and still runnin'. Good freight horses don't come cheap. All this, on top of reimbursin' people for all the stolen goods and money. Why, I've been robbed twice m'self, and Mist' Abbott has had to stand good for the losses. Just as well he's selling out."

"So the outfit is changing hands?"

Lysander nodded. "Yes'm, any time now. Railroad's coming through, so if the boss don't go broke before he can sell to 'em, he'd sure'n hell go broke trying to hang on and buck 'em. No matter how it's sliced, Flaming Geyser's days are numbered."

"And yours with it?"

Lysander bristled. "I'll get by. Always have."

Question is, Jessie thought walking away, *is* how *he's getting by.*

The restaurant across the street had a vertical sign hanging over its entrance: TIP TOP. Inside, the walls were simply lumber, ceiling and floor the same. There were no decorations whatsoever, no pictures or curtains; the tables were round, topped with peeling surfaces, and the seats were cheap, wire-backed ice-cream-parlor chairs.

Sheriff Maxwell was there having steak and eggs, and motioned for Jessie and Ki to join him. "This's the first food I've eaten since lunch yesterday," he said. "I was up'n gone afore dawn, trying to serve a logger with a bastardy paper."

"Did you get it served?" Ki asked.

"Well, yes. Finally." Maxwell turned over his hand and displayed a raw, deep cut across the palm. "He gave me a little tussle with his jack-knife first. I guess that's why I was a little late getting around to the body."

Jessie raised an eyebrow. "Body?"

"In the lane aside the depot. A man, didn't recognize him, sort of the hardcase drifter kind, shot neat'n clean at fairly close range. Not where he was found, though. Strangest thing. Located a rifle up on the depot roof, at the end overlooking the yard, that might've belonged to the de-ceased. It'd been fired, anyhow."

"How interesting."

"Ain't it, though?" Maxwell took a long sip of coffee, studying Jessie with veiled eyes. "If you don't mind answering, you think he might've had anything to do with the fire?"

"I do mind answering, but I will. I think it sounds, by the way you tell it, that he might." Jessie was hedging—and she had a sneaky suspicion that the sheriff knew it—but she was reluctant to confess her part in the gunman's death. To do so would require her to reveal more than she cared to, and there were too many ambushes and other mysterious menaces for her to trust anyone, even a lawman her gut instinct told her was honorable. "What do you think, Sheriff?"

"Simmer down." He paused while Jessie and Ki ordered breakfast, then went on. "Me, I don't cotton much to theories. I'll write it up as accidental and have the county pay for a buryin'. If later I'm proved wrong, why, it'll just have been accidental. Did you say y'sterday that you two were heading out somewheres?"

"I said we were going to the Delmonicos'."

"That's right. They're easy to get to. Take the north trail outta town for about three, four miles, and look for a big sawmill blade with their name on it. It's by the lane leading to their main camp. You going today?"

"Right after breakfast."

"Uh-huh. And where did you say you were coming from?"

"Take us or leave us," Jessie said. "But don't prod me around."

Suddenly, wonderfully, the sheriff was grinning.

Platters of eggs and dollar-sized hotcakes were served. As the three sat eating, there was a regular, almost constant procession of persons stopping by the table. Some chatted casually, some not so casually. The gist of all the talk came down to one thing. The current rash of mayhem and murder had Zenobia frightened.

Then a clatter of approaching hooves sounded in the street outside. Maxwell looked out the window and stiffened. "Blazes!" he growled. "Are the hellions coming to gun up the town?"

Glancing through the window, Jessie and Ki saw a dozen or so riders filing by. They were a grim-looking, ragtag bunch, some clad in buckskins, others in homespuns, all bristling with knives and pistols and longguns, aboard a motley collection of mustangers and mules. Trappers, no doubt about it—a wild, increasingly endangered species of Yanks, Brits, Canucks, Ruskies,'breeds, and even renegade Indians ousted from their tribes. When they had passed from view, Sheriff Maxwell sat back in his chair and stewed silently, waiting. It didn't take long. Evidently reining in at the sheriff's substation and not finding Maxwell in, they trooped along the street in search of him. Abruptly, their faces appeared in the glass of the restaurant window, peering in, and they piled through the door, bleak of face, stern of eye, intent on confrontation.

A big-bodied, great-bellied man, wearing garments of greased, worn hide, stepped to the fore. "You be the law?" he demanded.

"Toad-Eye Topes, you plumb well know I am," Maxwell replied. "What d'you want?"

"We come to report a matter," Topes said. "One of our company, Abel Bone, rode out past the trap lines early yesterday mornin'. He didn't show up last night."

"Well, what of it? You want me to go looking for him?"

"Don't need to, Sheriff. We went lookin' for Bone, and found him—what was left of him—shot in the back."

During the moment of tense silence following the startling statement, Maxwell, Jessie, and Ki all stared at the trappers.

"You sure about this?" Maxwell asked at length.

"We don't aim to make no mistake," Topes

replied. "And we want justice."

The sheriff sagged a little in his chair. "Everything is gettin' no better fast. Aw'ri', where was Bone's body found?"

"Nor'east, maybe six miles," the trapper answered. "He told Willie Renfrew here he aimed to ride the hills toward Mud Mountain. That's how we come to look for him thataway. We figured maybe he'd got lost or hurt hisself."

Ki spoke up, frowning. "A trapper, lost?"

Topes hesitated, glancing suspiciously at Ki.

"If he hadn't asked it, I was ready to," Maxwell responded, sounding resigned. "Answer up, Topes; that does seem a mite odd."

"Abel Bone, he wasn't really one of us in the usual sense," Topes replied uneasily. "From what he told us, he was raised in the Appalachians and headed west to California with gold fever. Prospector, y'see? Always swearin' trapping was only temporary, a way of earnin' his vittles till he made his big strike, but he'd been that way a good twenty years that I knowed of."

Nodding, Ki asked another question. "And the land out by Mud Mountain interested Bone?"

"Guess so," Tope allowed. " 'Course, like all prospectors, he was closemouthed about why he was curious over this spot or that."

Ki nodded a third time, thoughtfully. But it was Jessie who spoke up this time, asking, "Do you suppose that's why Abel Bone was killed?"

"Naw. He was kilt on account of crossin' Delmonico land. Them loggers hate us. Reckon they'd kill us all, if they got a chance."

"It don't always pay to jump at conclusions," Maxwell said.

"If the loggers didn't kill Bone, who did?"

"Well, I'll see if I can find that out, Topes. But what I've found out so far is that both sides up here are almighty busy accusing the other feller of skullduggery. Ever occur to you that you might be wrong?"

Jessie expected the trappers to explode in anger. They didn't. An exchange of glances went around the group. They seemed almost satisfied.

"Don't give it a second thought," Topes told the sheriff. "Maybe somebody else will take care of things."

Maxwell made no answer.

Topes said, "There are two kinds of lawmen, y'know. One kind is mighty good at serving papers and suchlike. The other kind catches backshooters."

"Mist' Topes," Maxwell said placidly. "I never heard you talk like that before. I always had the highest regard for you. Do I hear you apologize?"

Jessie blinked. The whole scene was so relaxed, almost friendly.

Topes seemed to think it over. "Yes," he said, and his voice was like sandpaper.

"Yes, what?" Maxwell said paternally, amiably.

"Yes, I apologize."

"You boys ride back to your digs," Maxwell said. "Don't go off half-cocked and start something you'll be sorry for later. I know how you feel, but nobody ever gained anything by sod-pawin'."

The trappers stared at him, muttered among

themselves. But finally Topes reluctantly growled, "Mind your hair"—a trapper's farewell meaning literally "watch your scalp"—and led his company out of the restaurant.

After the trappers had departed, Jessie asked the sheriff, "Are things as bad as we're hearing?"

"Worse," Maxwell allowed. "Bad ain't no name for it. There's the makings of a first-class feud hereabouts. Them trappers are salty loners, mostly from the Rocky Mountain country. Pack long rifles, as you saw, and know how to use them. Why, one of another timberland owner's jacks—Sheales's man—was bushwhacked in his timberland, and the slug that drilled the jack through the shoulder was fired from way up on a rimrock nigh a mile off."

"That's shooting by any standard," Jessie remarked.

"But the trappers won't have it easy if things do bust loose," Maxwell went on. "Loggers are plenty salty, too. Sheales's outfit, the Archer Brothers camp, the Peasleys, and the biggest, the Delmonicos . . . they've got an army of buckos rarin' to even the score."

"The score as the loggers see it, you mean," Jessie said. "What Topes just asked about Bone's death is the same as what the loggers are asking—'If the trappers aren't responsible, who is?' "

"Eg-zactly." The sheriff regarded his coffee grimly. "I'm hoping maybe there'll be an answer to both questions before long, before it's too late . . ."

Leaving the restaurant, Jessie and Ki walked over to the stable and retrieved their horses.

The wagon trail north that Sheriff Maxwell had referred to intersected the main road a short ways from Zenobia. But before they rode out of town, they tracked down the telegraph office, which was not much more than a windowless shed abutting the general store. There, Jessie wired a short, encoded message to Val Gresham in Seattle, giving him instructions without explanations.

"I know it's a long shot, but if my hunch works," Jessie remarked as they remounted, "and Val follows through unquestioningly, he'll be due for promotion."

The trail north proved to be a meandering course, squiggling toward an increasingly rugged country of tumbling creeks and thickly forested slopes. The sun had just passed into midmorning when the trail funneled into a ravine, an elongated bottleneck that stretched some distance ahead before widening back out again. And all along the high ridges grew so many trees that the impression was of one single entity sheared down its middle by the bisecting canyon trail. Finally, the canyon began widening, its sides gradually leaning away and lowering as well. Only once, sharply and briefly, did they draw close together again, and then they seemed to converge almost into one unbroken cliff. It didn't quite, for it was there that Jessie and Ki spotted the signpost and secondary trail.

The signpost consisted of an old sawmill blade bolted to a proper-sized peeled log. It was set up beside the secondary trail, which cut away toward an easily overlooked canyon offshoot; painted on the blade was the name DELMONICO, and a hand whose finger pointed westward along the rutted lane.

Angling onto the lane, they capped a knoll and came to a meadowed slope. There two riders appeared, one erupting out of a slash, the other hammering down the slope, and converged on them. Both were husky, hard-featured jacks, packing handguns and carrying Winchesters in saddle boots.

One of them called, "You're on private land."

"We're heading for the camp," Jessie replied.

"Who're you?"

"Jessica Starbuck, and this's my friend, Ki."

The other man began, "Send 'em packin', Boss; they—"

"Yeah, yeah," the first one interrupted curtly, and turned back to Jessie and Ki. "Pleased to make your acquaintance. I'm Pierce Thorleigh, overseer of the Delmonico outfit. We . . . well, we'll just ride along with y'all."

The other jack didn't ride beside them; he rode slightly behind Ki, while in front Thorleigh fell in alongside Jessie. The overseer struck Jessie as the sort who didn't smile much as a rule, his face long, jut-jawed, thin-lipped. His long coat was open, revealing a plaid collarless shirt with a brass collar button at the throat, and cheap linsey-woolsey pants.

"You'll have to excuse our rough welcome," Thorleign remarked after a moment. "There's all sorts of trouble that ain't got sense to it. We've had gunsmoke and done some buryin'. So we're taking a close look at all strangers these days."

And that was the last he said until they reached the camp. Apparently he was as parsimonious with his words as he was with his trust, and Jessie felt no need to draw him out. The deeply rutted lane went pretty straight through some rock outcroppings and wooded groves, and she thought she could detect the noisy paralleling course of a hidden white-water tributary nearby. Soon the track began wandering in and out of steepening culverts and ridge-flanking groves, until finally it got tangled in a dense forest and dribbled to a halt at the far end of the forest.

A clearing was there, a big one hewn from the forest. The stream she'd heard ran through the middle, and next to it was a group of log buildings—bunkhouses, a cookhouse, a cache house, a wagon shed, and a corralled stable all forming a sort of street. Set apart on a slight knoll was a large cabin of the type known as "four-square," appearing to be a comfortable if ordinary box containing four or five rooms. Nothing appeared opulent or to have much paint on it, but it looked plush compared to the temporary tent camps the logging crews lived in when working the woods. Which was where they probably were now, Jessie guessed. They certainly weren't here, and neither was much of their equipment.

Dismounting by the main house, Thorleigh ordered the other jack to tend to their horses. The jack started walking the horses across to the stable, while they stepped to the porch and Thorleigh rapped the brass knocker on the front door. After a moment, the door was opened by a formidably proportioned housekeeper, with her gray hair pulled tight in a bun and a face to match.

"Mist' Delmonico," Thorleigh told her. "He's got visitors."

She ushered them inside the parlor, then disappeared. Jessie glanced about; there were Indian blankets strewn on the floor and hung against the walls, and the furniture was of the big, sturdy variety. This was a man's room, yet there were also antimacassars and bric-a-brac, indicating a feminine presence—probably that of Rod Delmonico's sister, Opal.

A tall, long-legged, wiry-bodied man strode into the room.

"Sorry to pester, Mist' Delmonico," Thorleigh said, "but we latched onto these folks, Miz Starbuck an' Ki, coming in from the main trail."

"Thanks, Pierce. You may go." Wearing a tan shirt, twill pants, and engineer boots, Delmonico was in his midthirties, Jessie estimated, and handsome in a craggy way. His nose was lopsided, and one ear was cauliflowered, evidently from some accurate fists in the past, and his mouth was a generous slash cut for good humor. It quirked pleasantly as he greeted her and Ki. "I'm sure glad you're here. And call me Rod, please, if I may call you Jessica."

"Jessie will do . . . Rod," she replied. "I trust we can be of service."

"If'n you don't mind my asking, wasn't it a mistake to give your name? Pierce Thorleigh's been with us for ten years, and has always proved trustworthy. Still, your coming here was to be secret."

"So secret that I was unaware that you knew." Jessie smiled dryly. "But just about everybody we've run across seemed to know we were on our way here." Quickly, she sketched what had happened to them in the pass, when the dying ambusher had called her by name.

"I don't understand it," Delmonico said heavily.

"A leak somewhere."

"But I don't see how, Jessie. Your man in Seattle, Val Gresham, wired me to expect you, but I m'self picked up the wire in Zenobia, and the telegrapher there is sworn to secrecy—and by all accounts, takes his swearin' seriously. I talked the matter over with Sheales, of course—"

"Who is Sheales again?"

"Yachats Sheales—" Delmonico pronounced it as "Yahahts"—"owner of a goodly chunk of timber tracts east of us, the other side of the main road. He's been suffering tribulations same as us. So we discussed the situation with him, naturally, but he's tight-lipped and reliable. Somebody must've overheard us talking; that's the only thing I can figure."

"It's possible," Jessie allowed.

"Sheales is here now," Delmonico said. "Me and my sister Opal have been talking with him out back on the porch, wondering when you'd get here."

Jessie and Ki followed Delmonico through the cabin and out a rear door, onto a tree-shaded wooden porch overlooking the stream. Delmonico introduced them to Sheales and Opal, who rose from where they were seated at a round table made from the crosscut slab of a huge tree. Sheales was a man of large build, bald, with a wide mattress of a beard spreading down his hefty chest. Jessie sensed a hint of swagger in his bearing, and a touch of worldly pride in his immaculately pressed tan coat and spotless dust-colored pants.

Opal Delmonico was about five feet seven, in her early thirties, and no hothouse beauty—her black hair was a bit frizzled, and her face was lined by years of toil. Yet her face also showed character, her lips full and her black eyes alert, and her figure curved in where it should and curved out where it should. She'd be, Ki reckoned, an interesting person to get to know.

Sitting down, Delmonico related what Jessie had told him, and her suspicion that someone was passing on information.

"That wouldn't surprise me any more'n everything else has," Sheales commented. "There's five, six operations in these hills, and there ain't none of us but what has to fight everything Nature throws against us. But this latest man-made storm has us flummoxed."

"How do you mean?"

Delmonico responded, "We can't figure it out, Jessie. Raiders will hit a camp at night and throw lead fast and loose. Then they ride away."

"A month ago, they hit my main camp," Sheales said. "They caught one of my jacks between the cook shack and the bunkhouse and killed him. When they rode off just before dawn, there wasn't a whole pane of glass left anywheres in the camp. They done the same thing to the others. Ain't no sense to it. I mean, it ain't like they're stealing anything, running off a herd of cows or something like that."

Ki asked, "Have you retaliated?"

Sheales eyed Ki as though he werc loco. "Have you ever tried to trap a trapper? Them gents are half snake, half buzzard."

"Then about three weeks ago," Delmonico went on, "my bookkeeper, Dion Nettle, went out with the payroll. Had a couple of the boys along guarding him. They didn't come back that night. When they weren't back by morning, I sent a crew to look for them. They didn't find Nettle, but they found the guys who'd been with him, with their throats slit; their horses shot, too, like the scene of a massacre. Nettle hasn't been seen since."

"You think he did it for the payroll money, or arranged to have it done?"

"Dion Nettle hasn't done anything wrong!" Opal spoke up, voice sharp with distress. "Not ever! He has to be found to clear his name."

"Nettle was engaged to marry Opal," Rod confided grimly. "Personally, I always thought he was a sober, hard worker, and marryin' Opal would've fixed him up pretty nice for the future. Last man on the place I'd expect to turn traitor, thief, and murderer."

"Things have happened since then, too," Sheales said. "F'instance, just a few days ago, one of Rod's riggers died when the spar tree he was on was powder-blasted out from under him. But this mystery concerning his bookkeeper is what convinced us to call on you Starbuckers for help."

"It's my opinion," Rod said, "that there's more to this than just a scrap between us and some trappers. Somebody's behind it all."

"And that somebody is not Dion Nettle!" Opal declared.

Ki asked, "Where did the butchery take place?"

"In a clearing over by Cedar Creek."

"I'd like to look over the ground there."

Jessie cast him a puzzled glance. "Whatever for?"

"I honestly can't say, Jessie, and I don't think it's worth both of us going. It's a place to start, is all. It also sounds like it was a messy confrontation, and in messes, sometimes clues get left behind."

Rod nodded. "I'll send a man along with you, Ki."

"No, thanks. Don't forget, there's a leak around here."

"Let me show you the way," Opal begged. "You're trying to save Dion's good name. I want to help."

"I'd rather you didn't. Somebody knew we were coming and tried to kill us, and there's no guarantee it won't happen again. Thanks, but I don't want to risk your life unnecessarily."

Rod sighed heavily. "Well, I'll give you directions how to reach the slaughterin' spot."

Yachats Sheales got up from the table. "I must be getting back to camp," he said. "Miz Starbuck,

Ki, ride over and see my place as soon as you can."

"Thanks. Glad to," Jessie replied.

"Fine. I'll be looking for you." Sheales, with a parting grin, turned and hastened from the porch.

Jessie got up then and paced around, while Rod took out a black-tobacco cheroot and set to smoking. Finally, Jessie sat back down, frowning thoughtfully.

"Can you trust all your men, Rod?" she asked. "Is there anyone you might have suspicions about? I can't help thinking there well may be a spy on your place somewhere."

"I hate to think so, but I suppose it's possible. I've no idea who, though."

"This Sheales?"

"Yachats's owned his tract for a number of years. Quiet sort of a man. Not too neighborly."

"Prosperous?"

"Had a hard time lately, like all of us. But I believe he's meeting his payroll and other payments. He wasn't for sending for help at first, figured we oughtta fight it out ourselves. But he changed his mind overnight and said to send for you."

"Well," Ki said, "I'll get busy, if you'll give me directions."

"And while my brother is doing that," Opal told Jessie, "I'll show you to our guest rooms, and have your bags brought in. Take your pick. The rooms are quite Spartan, but they've a certain charming warmth . . ."

Soon, with Rod Delmonico's directions fresh in mind, Ki headed for the stable. He located his horse in the adjoining corral, but there was no sign of a hostler or other hands around, so he led his horse into the stable, found his gear, and began saddling up. He was just cinching up when an old man in bib overalls so new you could still see the bundling-cord marks on them sauntered into the stable. He squatted just inside the entrance, just squatted there, small, wiry, hair and drooping mustaches white, and stared with eyes that took in Ki to his roots. Until Ki got fed up and walked over to inquire just who'n hell the old man thought he was.

"Call me Upwind," the man replied, "Upwind Muldoon. I hear tell they call you Ki, and that your ladyfrien' is none tuther than Miz Starbuck herself."

"News travels fast."

"I might have some more news for you."

"I'd appreciate that."

"Funny situation here," Muldoon declared, still squatting. "Dion Nettle was going to marry Opal Delmonico. But Pierce Thorleigh, he wants to marry into the Delmonicos. Nettle disappears sudden and mysterious-like. Chip Russert knew something—"

"Who?"

"Chip Russert, one of the riggers. Chip for 'chipmunk,' on account of how he could climb trees. Russert knew something, I reckon, and Thorleigh knew that. So Russert, he dies when his spar is blown out from under him. Now him and Nettle are out of the way. Opal can't marry Nettle, so maybe Thorleigh'll have a chance. Savvy?"

"Yeah."

Muldoon stood, dusted off his new overalls. "Don't tell nobody I told you," he cautioned in a whisper, and strolled away.

Shaking his head, Ki went back to saddling his mount.

Riding out, Ki headed cross-country, following Delmonico's detailed directions. His route forged through stony gulches, flinty hogbacks, and thick but spotty groves of brush and timber. Maintaining a slow yet steady gait for more than an hour, he eventually reached the lip of a gorge that was steeply sloped, hopper-shaped, and heavily overgrown with pine and scrub, with a fairly wide stream curving out from the mouth. Cedar Creek, he judged.

As he continued toward the stream, his way grew rougher, like a washboard, and narrower, with encroaching vines and briars. Between him and the creek, some distance to his left, were a number of groves with similar undergrowth choking the spaces among the trees. He angled toward them, keeping in mind the landmarks Delmonico had told him would pinpoint the clearing where Dion Nettle's escorts had met their grisly fate.

Nearing the area through dense brush, Ki caught the stench from the carcasses of the slain horses. Though the animals had been shot three weeks before, and the buzzards had no doubt been busy, the odor remained. The reek served to guide him, contrary to his roan's obvious wishes to head elsewhere, and presently they came upon a path. It was hardly more than a single-file ribbon where passing hooves had beaten the ground raw, but according to Delmonico, it traversed the clearing. So, turning onto it, Ki forced his horse into a trot. After a bit the path looped in a kinky S-curve, passed through a fringe of trees and boulders, and entered the clearing.

Tall grass, scrub, and thickets of aspen, fir, and pine pressed close along the sides of the clearing, hindering the sight of anyone coming or going. Midway through, the path showed a big blotch, as though something dark had spilled and soaked in there. Along both shoulders were the remains of the horses, mostly bare bones now, and as Ki approached, a few buzzards arose and lazily flapped away.

Dismounting, Ki secured his horse to a tree off-trail and then went to the dried pool of blood. There he stood, gradually turning around while his dark eyes searched every inch of the gritty path within sight. There wasn't much to find, not after three weeks of intermittent rain and wind—the odd bootmark, a handful of spent .45 shells, some traces of tobacco and paper where someone had tossed a cigarette butt—and perhaps they meant nothing anyhow. Rod Delmonico and his men had been here, too, after the slaughter. But Ki kept searching, moving over to check around the carcasses, hoping to locate something that could be called a clue.

Finally, discouraged, he turned to retrieve his horse. It was getting on in the afternoon by now, the sun hovering above the tree line, but the low angle of its rays chanced to reflect off of something metallic. Ki hastened to see what it was. It was on the ground beneath the bones of one of the horses—the steel blade of a knife. Perhaps when Delmonico and his men had visited this spot, the horses' bones had not been picked clean by the buzzards, and the knife, under the carcass, had not been seen—

Or so he was thinking when somebody shouted, "Ki!"

Ki leaped up, pivoting, then froze.

Four men, walking abreast, approached along the path from the far side of the clearing. They were tough enough to make ordinary tough, say one of Delmonico's jacks, look like a gentleman. It wasn't their clothes, which weren't much even for a drifter, and these men sort of had the feel of drifters about them, but there was just a chill of the inhuman and merciless about them. The first was wolf-jawed, yellow teeth to match, a long nose and slitted eyes. The second was very young, and the very young could be crazy-dangerous, Ki knew. The third and fourth looked like squat, furry-throated apes, identical twins, perhaps. The wolf-jawed man was apparently the leader.

He said, "Uh-uh, don't move."

Ki cringed, slumping pathetically. "Wh–what're you going to do, fellows? Hey, I ain't got nothing, honest."

The young'un sneered mockingly. "Ain't got no gun, Chinee-boy?"

"No guts to use one," one of the apes quipped snidely.

"Betcha he's got somethin', Fritz. All them Chinks got hatchets and stuff hidden on 'em." The other ape swaggered up to Ki and snickered. "In his vest, I betcha. You, take off your vest."

"Sure, sure, anything you say," Ki whined, fumbling at the buttons, surreptitiously palming a *shuriken* from one of the pockets. "Just don't hurt me. You won't hurt me, will you?"

The men laughed contemptuously.

As Ki let his vest fall to the ground, the wolf-jawed man shouldered forward and raised his long-barreled Colt .45, pressing its muzzle against Ki's forehead. "I'm doing you a favor, boy. I'm gonna make a big, round eye smack-dab in the middle of your two squinty slits."

It was the last move he made. Before the wolf-jawed man could squeeze the trigger, Ki rammed the heel of his hand to the man's temple in a *teisho* blow, fracturing his skull like an egg and driving shards of broken bones into his brain. The wolf-jawed man died on his feet. Simultaneously, Ki kicked out with his right foot, first catching the ape in front of him in the kneecap; then, as the ape began crumpling, Ki brought his leg up square in the man's balls—hard, rendering him unconscious.

The pair of bodies in front blocked the other ape and the young gunman from blasting Ki at point-blank range. Before the two had fallen, Ki sent the *shuriken* speeding toward the young'un, even while he was diving the short distance toward the ape. Using a forward snap kick, followed by a sideways elbow smash, Ki caved in the man's ribs and stopped his heart. The man fell to his knees, mimicking the young'un, who'd crumpled hunched over as though he was praying, the *shuriken* protruding from his blood-spurting larynx.

With a stony if disgusted look, Ki eyed the four for signs of life, then left them where they lay to go pick up his vest. Next, he went back to the carcass and retrieved the knife. It was of a fairly standard hunting variety, similar in blade to a Bowie, with the sort of bone handle that looked he-man sportin' in the store, but tended to become brittle and loosen given time and usage. On one side of the handle, near the haft, Ki spotted initials carved in the bone: PT.

PT—Pierce Thorleigh.

Purse-lipped, Ki made a closer inspection of the ground around all the carcasses, but discovered nothing more. Nor did he turn up anything when he made a quick rifling of the four bodies. Perhaps, he thought as he headed for his horse, Delmonico or one of his men would be able to recognize the dead killers, or find a clue if and when they located the killers' horses, which must've been stashed somewhere nearby. In any case, as soon as he returned to the main camp, he'd request a party and wagon be sent out to collect the corpses.

But news about the knife could wait for now, Ki decided, placing it carefully into his saddlebag.

★

Chapter 6

It was just sundown with the western sky still light when Ki arrived back at the Delmonico camp. Lamps burnt in the main cabin and a couple of the bunkhouses, and as Ki dismounted by the stable, a billow of sparks rose from the cookhouse stovepipe, indicating someone had just added wood to the fire. The yard appeared as deserted as before—he assumed whatever hands were around were in the cookhouse or bunkhouses—but from the stable barn came the sounds of a blacksmith hammering. He led his roan into the stable, where the blacksmith helped provide it with a rubdown and feed, before letting it out into the corral.

Going to the main cabin, Ki found Jessie, both Delmonicos, and Pierce Thorleigh conversing in the parlor. Through an open door, the housekeeper could be seen setting a clawfoot dining table, laying out silverware and the good china in honor of the guests. Savory odors wafted out from the kitchen, indicating supper was about to be served.

"I hate ruining everyone's appetite," Ki said, then recounted his run-in at the clearing. He finished by giving Jessie a quick, slightly sad smile and adding, "Shouldn't have killed them."

"Don't regret it," Jessie said. "I don't."

"At least I spared one of them." Ki paused, sighed. "Well, what's done is done."

"And once done, one moves on," Thorleigh said heavily. "Speakin' of moving on, Mist' Delmonico, I was just about to go, anyway. I'll have some of the boys hitch up a wagon and mule team, and we'll fetch in the bodies. 'Tween us, I vouch we know every man in every camp and town around. If we can't identify the dead'uns, they're strangers hereabouts f'sure."

Grim-visaged, the overseer hastened out.

Then Ki said, "I mean it. I should've held back, kept one of those killers alive to ask a few questions. Like how'd they know to wait for me, that I was going there. No mistake that they did; one called me by name."

Opal gasped. "That leak again!"

"But I can't see how!" Rod countered. "Did you chance to talk to anyone besides us?"

"No," Ki replied; then, remembering Upwind Muldoon, he added, "Not about where I was riding."

"Well, that leaves only us and Yachats Sheales. But he wouldn't have told, had no reason to."

"At least nobody can blame Dion for it," Opal said, somewhat forlornly. "Really, this's more than I can bear. I think I should call off my birthday party. It's only three days from now, and the folks we've invited will be disappointed; they've been making plans to come, some from miles away, but . . . oh, I don't know what to do."

Jessie had been pacing near an open side window. Suddenly, her head jerked up and she seemed to be listening. "Have the party," she urged, quietly drawing her pistol. "It may give us a chance to look everybody over."

"Very well, I'll have the party—*eek!*"

Opal screamed as Jessie suddenly, unexpectedly, ducked her head and shoulders out the window, aiming her pistol at some unseen target.

"You!" Jessie snapped. "Hold it!"

Ki, Rod, and Opal sprang to the window, where they spotted a man crouching a short distance away against the side wall.

"What're you doing there?" Rod demanded.

"Why—why," the man stammered, "Pierce Thorleigh told me to clean away the grass and trash from around the cabin."

"He did, did he?" Rod growled. "We'll find out mighty soon whether you're lyin' or not!"

"Who's this man?" Jessie asked.

"He's one of the jacks," Rod answered, climbing out the window. He went over to the jack, a slightly stoop-shouldered man with dull eyes and, at the moment, a case of the shakes. "What're you frightened about? Got a guilty conscience?"

"No, sir. It's, ah, she scared me. I was just going to start cleaning up—"

"Without any tools?" Ki asked, joining Rod.

"I was going to see what I'd need, then go and get them."

From the window, Jessie commented, "You talk quite well for a logger."

"I've had schooling, ma'am," the man answered. "Needed a job, so I took the only thing offered. Besides, I don't happen to be much of a jack."

Rod gave a snort. "C'mon; we're going to see Thorleigh."

He and Ki marched the jack along to the front of the cabin, where Jessie and Opal met them coming out the door. Together, they continued on to the stable, the jack increasingly nervous. When they reached the stable entrance, Rod yelled, "Pierce!"

Thorleigh emerged, wiping his hands on a rag. "Them mules get ornerier—"

"Never mind that! Did you give this man some orders?"

"Sure," Pierce said. "Told Gilbert here to spruce up around the cabin, make it nice'n tidy for Miz Opal's party."

"All right." Rod turned to the jack. "Get your tools and get to work."

The man hurried away, plainly relieved.

"Anything wrong, Mist' Delmonico?" Thorleigh asked.

"We found him outside the cabin, acting sneaky and scared. Thought he might be snoopin' on what we was saying inside."

"Gilbert?" Thorleigh smiled. "He wouldn't understand what he heard, anyway."

Jessie's eyes narrowed. "That's strange. The man expresses himself well, and he said he'd been to school."

"I don't know much about him." Thorleigh shrugged. "His usual job is saw-filing. Now, if you'll excuse me, I've got some mules needin' hitchin'."

With that, Thorleigh started back inside the stable, and Rod and Opal began heading toward the cabin. Jessie, catching a glance from Ki, paused while he said to the Delmonicos, "You go on ahead. We'll be along in a minute, just want to check on our horses."

Puzzled, Jessie went with Ki into the stable. Catching up with Thorleigh, Ki said, "Have you a good, sharp knife, Pierce? I need to bore a hole in my saddlebag belt over here."

It seemed to Jessie that Thorleigh looked startled. But he went along with them to the tack area, where Ki had put his saddle, bags, and gear on a sawhorse. Thorleigh took a knife out of his pants pocket, a two-bladed jackknife, and handed it to Ki.

"This's a pretty small knife for a logger to use," Ki remarked. He opened his saddlebag and brought out the bone-handled hunting knife he'd found under the carcass. "Isn't this yours?"

Thorleigh's eyes bulged at the sight of it. "Yeah!" he exclaimed, and quickly demanded, "Where'd you find it?"

"Out at the clearing where those men were killed. Somebody dropped it there."

"I'll be damned! Dion Nettle borrowed that knife

from me the day he went away and never came back," Thorleigh explained, adding slowly, "so that proves it: Dion was there with them. It'd break Miz Opal's heart if she knew."

It was Jessie who answered. "We won't tell her."

With a nod, Thorleigh went back through the stable toward the corral, to join his men in hitching a mule team to a wagon.

Jessie and Ki headed back to the cabin. "And to supper," Ki said. "If I'm not mistaken, that was a pot roast I smelled." While crossing the yard, he related his brief conversation with Upwind Muldoon, concluding with, "I don't know if there's anything to what Muldoon had to say, Jessie, but he clearly has it in for Pierce Thorleigh. It could be that they brawled once, or Muldoon's been around here so long he thinks he owns the place."

"No, I doubt it's resentment," Jessie replied. "While you were out this afternoon, Rod filled me in about some of his hands. Muldoon's an old-timer, all right, but not here. He wandered in only about three years ago, and Rod gave him a job because he's tops at mending bridles, saddles, and harnesses. So maybe he has good reason to dislike Thorleigh. How do you size up the overseer, and his answers about his knife? Do you think he's our spy?"

"I'm not ready to call him crooked," Ki said. "He's worth keeping under suspicion, though, as is everyone else. If we watch him closely, we might see if he's with one man more than the others, and all that. If Thorleigh should be traitoring, he must have a messenger . . ."

Ki was not disappointed about supper. Rod Delmonico sat at the head and his sister at the foot of the clawfoot table, which groaned under the weight of all the food. Nothing more was said about the murderous situation, but Opal kept urging Ki to have another helping of this dish or that, and Ki made a valiant effort to prove his appreciation of the cooking by eating fair to bursting.

As for Jessie, she, too, decided the dinner was a marvel, particularly considering it was out here on the wild hind end of nowhere. And Rod—his manner gracious and outgoing, his conversation shrewdly probing—had confirmed her initial impression of him as an intelligent, educated man deeply concerned with the welfare of his sister and crewmen. She could now add to that a sense of personal attraction, a budding awareness that bordered on sexual arousal. Not that she had any such designs in mind, she thought hastily; her mission was strictly business and that was how it'd be, uncomplicated.

Afterward, they enjoyed snifters of brandy, Rod smoking another of his cheroots, and then they broke up for the night, Jessie and Ki going to their respective rooms. When Opal had remarked that the guest rooms were Spartan, she hadn't been kidding: Jessie's was about the size of a monk's cell. Still, there was also a charm and warmth about it, with a bright Indian weaving serving as the bedspread, and a vase of freshly picked wildflowers on the bureau.

Although it was still relatively early, Jessie for one was glad to retire; she was tired and wanted to think, especially about what Upwind Muldoon had told Ki. She had heard of situations like that before—a *segundo* wanting to inherit an outfit through marriage. If goaded enough, such an ambitious man would not hesitate to remove others to clear the way for himself. Indeed, if there were any truth to Muldoon's story, what was more natural than for Pierce Thorleigh to be the spy here? Rod Delmonico might not have told him everything, but he was in a position to learn all he needed to by eavesdropping. And it would be easy for a man of Thorleigh's standing and influence to get ahold of men to ambush her and Ki at the pass, intent on killing them before they could reach the camp. Yes, Thorleigh could have planned it all. But there was a flaw in this line of thought: it failed to explain the deadly trouble Quinn Abbott and his Flaming Geyser line were in, and Jessie couldn't shake the hunch that the problems were somehow connected.

"I don't like this business," she murmured, sitting down on the side of the bed, adding as she pulled back the coverlet, "not any of it. I can scent more trouble on the way, and when it does come, it'll probably be an avalanche."

Suddenly, she bent forward and pulled something from under the edge of her pillow, a piece of soiled paper that read:

Remember Wyoming and the Pascal gang? One you didn't catch is here. My revenge will be more than a bullet. I am alone in this. I'll get you, bitch, and torture you to death. You have walked into my trap.

As Jessie read the scrawl, her mind went back to the case of Oscar Pascal, which she and Ki had solved the previous year. Pascal, a crooked sheriff, and a gang of gunmen had led a reign of terror, rustling and horse thieving and murdering at will. She and Ki had unearthed their plot to defraud the Army and send an innocent rancher to jail. In the final showdown, Pascal and his gang had died or been caught and sentenced to prison. She had always thought that one or more of the group had escaped, though. Now it seemed that she had been right.

For this scrawl to be true, one of the old gang was here in the Delmonico logging operation. Jessie would not be able to recognize him, and the man could watch for an opportunity to settle accounts. She'd have to be on guard against this new threat even while she was looking into the Delmonicos' problems.

Just as she was putting the note into her shirt pocket, a tentative knock sounded on her door. "Jessie? It's me, Rod. Are you . . . ?"

"Oh, yes, I'm decent. Come on in; the door's unlocked."

The door eased ajar and Rod Delmonico slid inside, quietly closing the door behind him. "I wanted to make sure you were safe," he said. "Among other things." He padded across the room in stockinged feet and checked behind the drapes, then knelt beside her to peer under the bed. "Well, I'd say you're safe now, Jessie."

Jessie, still sitting on the bed, smiled down at him, admiring his husky torso, suntanned face, and vivid eyes . . . and wondering a little about the faint bulge along one trouser leg. "Oh, I'm not so sure of that."

"Sure?" Rod settled on the bed alongside her. "Not sure of what?"

"I'm not sure that I'm safe now, not with you here."

"You're absolutely not," he declared, rubbing his hands along the calves of Jessie's boots. "Still, who's to know who's safe from whom? The doors are made of thick planks, and the walls are of logs. We can be quite ourselves."

"Rod, what're you doing?"

What he was doing was removing her boots. In one fell swoop, he slid them off and began massaging her bare feet. Startled, Jessie sat straight up, feeling his lips caressing her toes.

"Stop it, Rod. Rod?"

"You're a goddess," he murmured, his lips gentle.

Jessie felt a perverse response, an intriguing tingle worming through her flesh. "Well, this goddess is tired. Very tired and very dirty."

"Good. Goddesses are more fun when they're mortal." He rose and extended his hands. "Come; your bath has been drawn."

"A bath? You didn't!"

"You're right. The housekeeper did, just before retiring to her room. You don't think I'd let a filthy creature sleep in a clean bed, do you?"

Laughing, Jessie allowed Rod to pull her upright. Barefoot, she followed him out to the end of the hallway, where a sort of alcove abutted the kitchen. Rod opened the pineboard door, bumping against Jessie with his manhood as he held it wide for her. She thought dizzily, *Either Rod's got a tree trunk down his leg, or he's hung like a mule!*

The bathroom consisted of a marble-topped cabinet, a cane-bottomed chair with two towels folded neatly on it, a small frosted-glass window, and a roll-rim zinc tub. The tub was filled with steaming water, with a wire-mesh holder hooked over the rim containing a washcloth and a bar of yellow soap.

"I can't wait to dive in," Jessie said, and started to unbutton her blouse. When Rod didn't take her hint to leave, she stopped, but said nothing more as he latched the door behind them and moved closer to her.

"Jessie . . ."

"No, Rod. Please go."

"Are you afraid?"

"I'm tired, I told you."

"I'll wake you up."

"That's what I'm afraid of." And it was the truth, for she felt this to be the wrong time and the wrong place. She feared that letting things progress might ruin the good working relationship they had, which was based on respect and a sense of equality. She also knew the urgent demands of a hungry body, and she was strong enough to resist pure lust. What she was having a difficult time defying was the inexplicable flowing gentleness as he reached out and grasped her forearm; it was a light touch, but it affected her senses like a bow being drawn across violin strings.

"Let me," he said. "I want to."

His dexterous fingers began working on that same blouse button. Jessie felt mesmerized, unable to fight him even if she'd wanted to, and stood transfixed as he peeled her blouse off. Rod grinned, staring at her bared breasts and jutting nipples. Then he knelt and unfastened her jeans. He pushed them down, and she stepped out of them, leaving them puddled on the floor. Her drawstring drawers were edged with Valenciennes lace, and were of a fabric more translucent than her blouse. Rod had an intriguing ringside view of the golden delta between her thighs as he untied the drawstring and eased her drawers down her legs.

"You are truly a beautiful woman." He drew her hips toward him and kissed her upper thigh. "Thanks, Jessie, for letting me."

Slowly, he rose, and there was an impact as their bodies slid together. Her arms curled around his neck, her hardening breasts pressing against his chest, and her mouth insistent and bruising against his. He moaned slightly, deep in his throat, his hands gliding down her back to cup and stroke her tensing buttocks, until Jessie found that she was moaning a little, too.

Breaking their embrace, she laughed lightly, rich color in her face as she stepped into the tub. He caught her hand to support her as she slowly slid into the water and then stretched out in voluptuous enjoyment.

Rod stood watching her with a wide, satisfied smile.

"You liked undressing me, didn't you?" she asked.

"Yeah, I did."

"Fine. Come in and scrub my back, then. There's room."

Rod tore at his clothing. Jessie eyed his naked form as appreciatively as he'd studied hers. His shoulders were wide, his hips lean, and the muscles across his torso looked like the firm ridges of a washboard. And she noticed with something akin to trepidation that it definitely had not been a tree trunk in his pants.

He climbed into the tub and settled down behind her. She leaned forward, gathering her tawny hair in her hands and holding it up against her head, feeling him lathering soap across the arch of her back. He squinched closer, to a more comfortable position, and she became aware of her buttocks brushing against his inner thighs . . . and then of something growing long and hard, nudging the base of her spine.

"Your back's clean," he said, moving his wet, soapy palms around to wash her breasts, paying particular attention to her nipples.

"Damn you, Rod!"

"Like wood chips, they are. Feels good, doesn't it?"

She squirmed, whimpering, leaning against

him. "You know, Rod, I . . . I'm not easy. I don't care to be had like a bitch in heat."

"No, Jessie, you're very selective. We're alike that way, just as we're both proud, determined people who know what we want and have the self-confidence to go after it and believe we're worth it. We're too similar, and have too much regard for those similarities, to waste each other's time with silly games or false modesty."

"You've got it all figured out, haven't you?"

"It's what I'm *feeling*, not thinking. But is that what you're thinking, that you're being had?"

"Rod," she purred, languidly stretching back to give him easier access, "if I'm being had, I'm letting it happen."

"Take the blame," he whispered in her ear. "I'll take the rewards." His hands slid up and down her legs and into her groin.

Jessie lounged with her legs slightly bent and spread, while Rod soaped and cleansed and stirred her to feverish arousal. The brush of kneading hands across her breasts, the feathers of his fingers stroking her swelling nether lips, his gentle kiss on the nape of her neck, all combined to evoke in Jessie an erotic fever, and she found herself hot and trembly when she finally suggested, "Let's go to my room."

"We could be seen. Let's do it here."

"Somebody might want a bath."

"Let 'em wait their turn."

"Damn me," she whispered, easing from his embrace to rise, squatting, his legs stretched between hers. Placing his taunting shaft against the opening of her moist sheath, she guided Rod into her with her own trembling fingers, then settled down, groaning with the rock-hard feel of him as he began his penetrating entry. Pushing downward, she feared she'd cry out and awaken everyone else in the cabin before he entirely buried up within her. God, he was filling her! And to relieve the strain she spread her legs wider, quivering as she continued to feel herself stretched by his massive shaft.

Rod chuckled at her erotic eagerness, slowly sliding between her flushed thighs, driving upward until he had burrowed all of him fully inside. Jessie could not control her reactions. She began riding his shaft up and down, only vaguely aware that he was gripping her on either side of her naked hips, that he was letting her loins do all the work.

But then he, too, started pumping, tunneling deeply, furiously, hammering her savagely. "This is nice," he gasped.

Jessie thought it was pretty good, too. She responded with equal savagery, her breasts trembling to his surging assaults, her body pulsing as she undulated her buttocks against his pelvis. Hooking her calves over the sides of the tub, she splayed her thighs to allow him greater access. He rubbed her crevice, his other hand massaging her breast, while she pumped smoothly upon his rod, matched rhythmically by his strokes pistoning into her loins.

"Yesss, this is nice," she echoed shakily. "How'd you know?"

"Well, I've always found it nice before."

"I mean, how'd you know I'd be willing?"

"I don't know," Rod replied, thrusting upward.

His vague answer seemed to satisfy Jessie, as a tremor began gathering inside her, a warning like the advance of a thundering avalanche. Frantically, she raced to meet it, her motions skewering her completely around his hammering manhood. She poised breathless, tensing, straining . . .

"Ahhh!" She bit her forearm to keep from screaming, her nails raking the rim of the tub. She felt Rod shuddering, and his seething eruption volcanoed up into her spasming belly. Then, collapsing limply, she lay panting, pressed firmly back against him, exhausted and satiated.

Soon, Jessie yawned and climbed from the tub. A twinge of self-consciousness stole over her as she toweled dry. "I wasn't kidding," she said, stifling a contented yawn. "I'm afraid I've had a grueling day, and now I'm really tired—"

A raucous yell and the crack of a gun sounded outside the cabin. The sensuous spell shattered, Rod leaped from the tub to the window, jerking it open to peer outside. "That's one of my sentries!" he blurted. "We're being attacked!"

For a split second, Jessie stared at his astounded face. Then she was springing one way, gasping, "Where's my shirt?" and Rod was springing the other. "Where's a towel?"

Dashing out of the bathroom before Rod, who was hopping on one leg with his pants half on, Jessie got to her room just before other bedroom doors started wrenching open. Ki, Opal, and the housekeeper appeared in the hall. Jessie snatched up her pistol, taking a moment to glance out her room's window, spotting a night-shrouded rider galloping into the camp from the direction of the wagon lane. Bellowing warnings, firing again into the air, the jack plunged his horse toward the nearest bunkhouse. As Jessie tugged on her boots, she could hear the muffled hoofbeats of a bunch of horses swiftly approaching the camp. The jack sprang from his horse and spanked it to running out of range, then sprinted to the bunkhouse door, where hands reached out to drag him inside.

By the time the bunkhouse door slammed shut, Jessie was out of her room and joining the others in the front room. Opal was in a short peignoir, the housekeeper was in a gunnysack of a nightgown, and Ki had on only his pants—as did Rod. They gave a quick acknowledgement of one another as Rod started passing out weapons and ammunition from a corner rifle cabinet. It was then, when grabbing the offered Winchester, that Ki noticed Rod's pants were soaked through, and Jessie had damp hair and a blouse plastered to her breasts. And he figured he'd better not ask a natural question like, "What've you been doing?" Besides, there wasn't time; the seige was on. The raiders, with a thunder of hooves, galloped into view, iron horseshoes bruising the hardpan of the lane.

In a rush they came, upward of twenty attackers pounding into the clearing, deploying about the camp, roaring salvos of gunfire into the cluster of buildings. The defending jacks responded full blast from the bunkhouses, lining their shots at the saffron flares that were winking in the darkness. Up in the cabin, Jessie, Ki, and the Delmonicos worked their Winchesters from four separate windows, while the housekeeper cannoned a blunderbuss of a shotgun out the kitchen door. In the flick of that sequence of seconds, the camp became a howling, rattling bedlam. The yells that rang out carried confusion and alarm, the raiders storming the bunkhouses and other structures with ferocity, yet seemingly caught a bit off-guard by the stout resistance they met.

Jessie, shifting position at her window, slipped on one of her empty cartridge cases. Regaining her balance, she broke out another glass pane for unhampered shooting, glimpsing two raiders going down under fire, slammed from their saddles. She levered her rifle for another shot, but the magazine was empty. Hastily, she started thumbing in fresh loads, hearing one of the raiders above the racket, evidently their leader, hurling curses and goading his men. The cabin began to reek of choking fumes, and a fog of powdersmoke thickened the air near the ceiling. Lead chewed constantly into the walls and through the windows, zipping and ricocheting about the rooms, as a number of raiders swung from their stirrups and charged the cabin on foot.

"Rush 'em!" their chief was commanding, no slouch when it came to fighting. "C'mon, you lazy bastards, wipe 'em out!"

But the five trapped inside kept his advancing gunhands respectful with swift, accurate fire. A man scurrying by Jessie's window abruptly let out a cry and clawed at his chest, spurting blood on his calfskin vest. The housekeeper let fly with her shotgun then, and as its thunderous discharge receded, wails and thrashings could be heard from where the men had retreated. At other windows, the Delmonicos and Ki were levering their rifles in rapid fire, Rod snarling oaths as he lambasted the dim figures of other advancing men. Nonetheless, time and again it appeared as if they were on the road to hell, as flying wedges of raiders would try to breach the front and back porches. And time and again, Jessie and the Delmonicos up front and Ki and the housekeeper in back laid waste to them through now weak-hinged doorways. Below, raiders assailed the cluster of buildings, only to have the steady whine of lumberjack bullets beat them back.

For a long time, the battle raged. But as dawn began to ooze across the eastern horizon, some of the shooting slowly died away. Finally, an eerie silence held the camp as a hint of sunrise gilded the sky.

"They got one more stab, I judge," Rod growled. "Daylight's too risky for the likes o' them to stick around. They've got to wipe us out now or pack it in."

"Speak of the devil," Opal snapped. "Here they come!"

Jessie and Ki saw that gunmen were bellying up from the sides and across the feebly lighted front of the knoll, apparently concentrating on the cabin because it housed the Delmonicos separate from the rest of the camp. A man, scuttling along beneath the windows, aimed and fired at Ki, but missed. Ki turned, ducking reflexively, just in time to see the man go down. Glancing over his shoulder, Ki gave Opal an admiring grin. She was using an old Remington conversion revolver now, and was handling it with effectiveness.

Suddenly, he shouted, "The door!"

The front door burst wide, nearly wrenched off its hinges by a wedge of burly gunmen all trying to claw in at the same time. Jessie and the housekeeper ran to defend the back door.

The clash was a brutal mess. Shots cracked; knives snicked; hands grappled for throats. Ki whacked his rifle across an evilly twisted face, almost bending the barrel as the man fell away in a spew of teeth and blood. Opal emptied her revolver, traded it for one a dying gunman had dropped, and emptied that, too. Then she clubbed with it while searching for a replacement. She accidentally kicked her brother as he wrestled with a gunman who was as raving mad as he; when next the gunman was glimpsed his head was near cut off, for Ki had drawn his short, curve-bladed *tanto* and was slashing at bellies and limbs with precise strokes.

Meanwhile, back in the kitchen, Jessie and the housekeeper riddled the door with bullets, but one defiant man managed to thrust halfway in, leering as he strove to trigger his pistol. There was a snick of steel as the housekeeper snatched up her butcher's cleaver from a cutting board and split open the man's skull. The man reeled backward, the cleaver still buried deep, his gory appearance causing a concerted shout from the stoop.

But the raiders were not done yet. As callous and vicious as they were, they still had hopes and promised wages to live for—the camp they were up against had nothing save inflamed desperation, and they were killing voraciously. The odds had evened mightily, the gang having suffered a fierce toll. Dead men lay across doorways, under windows, around the clearing. The morning air was overcast with pungent gunsmoke, fuming so strongly out of open windows that it appeared as though the interiors were burning.

At that moment, Pierce Thorleigh, four jacks, and their mule-driven wagonload of bodies rolled in.

It had taken the corpse collectors almost all night to go to the clearing and back because of the slow-moving mules and a wagon that could not travel directly overland. But now, in their own fashion, they attacked, Thorleigh and the two jacks on horseback fanning out from the lane while the wagon trundled straight in, the driver hurrawing the mules and his companion blasting away with a carbine. They struck the raiders on their flank, and three went down under the initial charge. Alarmed, the raiders hastily retreated, drawing away from the buildings and ceasing their attempts to overrun the cabin. They continued hazing with heavy fire, and their leader's ranting voice was drowning the others' shouts as he tried to establish authority, but the damage was done. His gunmen were milling wildly, those in the saddle starting to ride out, those afoot making a frantic dash for horses, slipping back into the habits common to hired killers: If at first you don't succeed, haul ass before it's shot off.

Sped on their way with blistering gun volleys, the surviving raiders spurred their horses out on the wagon lane, beating a retreat as fast as they could gallop. The rataplan of clicking irons faded swiftly into the distance.

Silence descended—a dry, sucked-out silence.

Slowly, Jessie, Ki, and the Delmonicos stepped out onto the front porch, scanning the camp. "They're on the run!" Opal cried, breaking the hush and laughing with shaky relief. "We stood them off, we did!"

"Not without a price," her brother morosely reminded her. As indeed was true. "A damn high price."

★

Chapter 7

In the aftermath, Jessie and Ki helped the Delmonicos take stock of the damage. The crewmen groaned and groused, for the fray had left them all aching with countless scratches, contusions, nicks, and bruises . . . as well as numerous sprains and chipped bones and minor bullet creases. Only two had suffered serious injuries—a left ear shot off, and a bullet through a left thigh—but four had died, though they had taken with them almost three times that many raiders. Unfortunately, those raiders had all been fatally wounded; a few hung on awhile, groaning deliriously, but none left were able to talk. And they proved as unidentifiable as the other outlaws who'd died before them—including, as it turned out, the ones the wagon had delivered.

Hours later, when the dead jacks were buried, the wounded jacks were tended and resting, and two wagonloads of dead raiders were en route to the sheriff in Zenobia, an utterly fatigued Jessie and Ki went to bed. Not surprisingly, they slept until quite late in the day. Finally arising, they found that Opal, too, had retired; she was still asleep, but Rod had stayed up, too concerned to rest.

He was out on the front porch, talking with a burly man whose jaw resembled a chunk of pickled beef—Bender Busch. And the lumberjack recognized his antagonist of two days before, for he stiffened and stared at Ki, his brows drawn together.

"Afternoon, Jessie, Ki," Rod greeted as they joined him. "This's Yachats Sheales's overseer, Bender Busch. They had a raid over there last night, too."

"Tell me about it," Jessie said.

"Same sort of thing," Busch replied. "They rode in fast and threw a ring of rifles around our camp before we knew what was happenin'. They holed us up tight until morning."

"Did they hit any other spreads, too?"

"Dunno, ma'am. I'm just reporting it, like Sheales told me to." Busch gave a halfhearted shrug, eyeing Jessie, then Ki. "Feller," he said to Ki, "I just want you to know I don't hold no hard feelings over what happened in town. After I got to thinking about it, I wasn't overproud of the whole business. Taking a swipe at that old jigger when he was on the ground wasn't such a sportin' thing to do, and I reckon if I hadn't been fit ready to bust, I wouldn't have done it. Y'see, it hadn't been too long before that we'd gotten raided, and I'd wasted a whole day trying to track where them blasted trappers had run to. When the first thing I saw when we hit town was a trapper swellin' around, I got my bristles up."

"Yes, imagine you had reason to go on the prod," Ki allowed.

After getting that matter off his chest, Busch appeared to be in a more sociable mood. "Well, s'long. Mist' Delmonico, if I don't see you again before, I'll see you at Miz Opal's party." With a final nod, Bender Busch turned and walked to his horse, which was tied to the hitchpost.

Purse-lipped, Jessie watched thoughtfully as Busch rode off. She then asked Rod, "Am I to understand that whenever a camp like yours is raided, other camps get raided at the same time?"

"Well, more'r less," he answered. "Not everybody gets hit as heavy. Them timber wolves sort of take their spite out on one spread."

"So the other camps get just enough trouble to keep them tied down, is that it?"

"I suppose that's it, Jessie, though I never thought of it that way. But why would they do it? What's behind it all?"

"I don't know, Rod," Jessie replied and tugged at her earlobe. "But I think a trip to Zenobia might be in order. I was planning to go there today anyway, probably stay over two or three days. This time nobody except you knows we're going, so there shouldn't be a leak. Even if there is, there won't be time to have a killer wait in ambush for us."

Jessie and Ki hastily packed bags for their quick trip, then went to the stable. They found old Upwind Muldoon sitting on a bench there, fiddling with a saw file.

Muldoon said, "You remember what I hinted?"

"Sure," Ki replied. "You got anything else to hint?"

"Maybe." Muldoon looked at them carefully, though his eyes were glued half-shut with sticky yellow matter, and put down the file to take a little snuff.

There were three ways of taking snuff. The original style, that of sniffing the powdered tobacco, was long out of fashion. The common method now, the run-of-the-mill method, was to take a pinch of snuff, pull out the cheek, and deposit the pinch in the little pouch between the gum and the inner skin of the cheek. There was another method, too, and this was the method the old man used. He took a pinch and rubbed it vigorously into his gum. This was the quickest and most effective method. It burnt worse than fire. It was the true addict's method.

He asked, "Did you hear about the raidin' last night over at the Sheales camp?"

"Bender Busch told us," Jessie said.

"Well, sir," Muldoon went on, ignoring her, "I was part of the crew who went collecting them bodies near Cedar Creek. On the way, I seen Thorleigh ride off from us. Where he went, I wouldn't know, but he was gone a long time. Caught up with us on the way back, he did."

Ki said, "You don't like him much, do you?"

"I hate his guts," Muldoon admitted without hesitation. "He's too uppity. Keeps tellin' me to stop loafin' and get to work. There ain't a man in this land can sharpen better'n me, if I'm left alone. He's a nagger, that's what, and I hate his guts."

"Thanks. Keep us posted if any more hints strike you," Ki said, and headed on into the stable with Jessie.

"If you're goin' for a ride, watch out for y'selves," Muldoon urged.

Jessie and Ki saddled up, cantered out to the lane, and hurried along it. About the time they got to the wagon trail to Zenobia, Ki spoke up. "Y'know, Thorleigh might've been telling the truth about lending Dion Nettle his knife. And maybe that jack you caught by the cabin *was* only following orders, and not eavesdropping."

"What about Thorleigh's mysterious ride last night?"

"That could've been innocent enough."

"He couldn't in that time have ridden to any camp except Sheales's," Jessie pointed out. "There's no other camp near enough. If he didn't go there, he probably rode out to tip someone off about something, such as us staying over at the Delmonicos and the smaller number of jacks who'd be there on hand. A man like Thorleigh wouldn't just ride around for the fun of it."

"True," Ki admitted. "Well, maybe he went to Sheales's place for something."

"We'll find out before this's over," Jessie vowed. "You don't seem to think that Thorleigh's a wrong one."

"Sometimes when evidence piles up against a man, it's best to look somewheres else for the guilty one," Ki answered. "And to boot, that Upwind Muldoon doesn't have all his lamps lit. He hates Thorleigh, and snoops around more than suits me."

"He's old, and not overly bright," Jessie agreed. "But there is a spy around the Delmonico camp, that's plain enough. And he must be caught. And there seems to be another angle, Ki—a personal angle for me." She told him now, for the first time, about the scrawled note she had found in her bed.

Ki's face grew stiff and wooden; to Jessie, it looked dangerous. "I'll be with you like glue. No telling who the lobo might be who's after you, and no telling when he might take a shot at you and hang it on the trappers."

"I'll be careful," Jessie promised. "Let's hit it up some . . ."

They continued on to Zenobia at a fast trot, enjoying the tag end of the pleasantly cool day. Jessie hoped the day's weather indicated a night that would be clear and moonlit, yet she was also aware that this was the season of quick storms and rain squalls. And on the northwestern horizon, there seemed to be a suspicious gray edge like a stagnant scum line.

The sheriff's office looked dim and empty inside as they passed on their way to the livery. Nor, as it turned out, was Sheriff Maxwell to be found around town; evidently, he was out somewhere on business. Jessie wished to speak with him, but obviously it had to wait. And it was probably a good thing, too, because of who else was in town.

There was a horse-and-buggy parked in front of the Flaming Geyser depot. Actually, the buggy was of the larger sort called a road wagon, with a padded seat, sixteen-spoke wheels, and a tailgated shortbed. This one had a dirty black body with stripes and red gear, and emblazoned along the side panels was the name MARMONT TIMBER CO. "Remember, Ki?" Jessie said. "That logger, Marmont, was the one who was told to deliver a cash shipment a day earlier than it was supposed to go out."

"Apparently he's doing just that."

"That's just what I was hoping," Jessie said, "and why I wanted to get to town today. This's luck, though, seeing it confirmed."

After stabling their horses, they were walking toward the Neskowin Inn when they saw the wagon heading out of town, Marmont himself at the reins. "That means," Jessie reckoned, "that the cash is now under the care of Sherwin Lysander, locked securely away for the night in his depot safe."

"Not," Ki added cryptically, "if our luck holds . . ."

An overcast dusk had settled by the time they checked into the hotel and ate dinner. By eight o'clock, the night had become velvet black.

“So much for our luck holding,” Jessie noted. “If anything does happen tonight, we likely won’t be able to see it.”

Ki nodded. “And if it starts raining so that we can’t move quickly, that’ll make things just dandy.”

They were in the tall brush behind and to one side of the depot, at an angle where the fenced yard did not interfere with watching the building. Their mounts were saddled and standing with dropped reins ready to go, a few feet away. One by one, the lights in town went out. The hours slipped into one another, and nothing happened to break the monotony of silence and darkness. Ki judged it to be about midnight when the wind rose. Presently, there were thunder and streaks of lightning away to the north. The storm was on its way.

Suddenly, Jessie’s mare threw up its head. Stepping back quickly, Jessie put her hand over its nose to prevent any whinnying while she listened intently. She could hear nothing. Then Ki gestured toward the depot, and she saw that a crack of light had appeared under the back door. Abruptly, the light disappeared. She heard the door opening.

Now a blacker shape moved in the dark, a horse stepping before the door. Its rider had already dismounted, and there was a faint rustle, as of someone passing into the depot. Their straining ears caught a faint click as the door closed.

Motioning for Jessie to stay and quiet the horses, Ki eased noiselessly forward. Reaching the door, he patted the saddle horse—an unkempt splotched grulla—ducked under its neck, and came up against the wall of the building. The light beneath the door had reappeared. Slowly, slowly turning the knob, then releasing it just as slowly, he left the door ajar a half-inch. He bent his head close to the casing and listened.

"I put the stuff in these two manila envelopes for you. That'll make it easier to carry in your saddlebags." The words were spoken in a whisper, but Ki recognized the gravelly voice of the agent, Sherwin Lysander.

"Aw' ri'," another voice said—a voice Ki had heard before, but at the moment couldn't quite identify. "But seal 'em good an' tight. If I was to lose so much as a dollar, the boss would cut my balls off. He's always hollerin' about some damn thing or—"

"Quit *your* hollering," Lysander admonished. "You're talking too loud. Besides, as long's you get your cut, you shouldn't worry. This beats chopping down wood, don't it?"

"You're a hot one to gripe!" the other retorted bitterly. "You got a soft snap. You just dink around here and get your graft."

"You better be on your way," the agent advised curtly, "or you won't get yours."

Silently closing the door, Ki slipped back to where Jessie waited with the horses. After he'd briefed her on what he'd overheard, they swung into their saddles just as the door opened. The light had again been put out. There were a few softly murmured words while Lysander and the other man worked at the saddlebags. Jessie and Ki could catch only "You all set?" and Lysander's answer: "You bet, Mac."

Leaning over, Ki whispered to Jessie, "Now I recollect who he is. Mac—that gent with the two-gun kid who tried to warn us off back in Orting."

The gunman, Mac, mounted and rode away from the depot. But Jessie and Ki had to sit still, for the door had not closed again. Lysander couldn't be seen, but, as Jessie figured, "he must be standing there, listening." Eyes and ears strained, they waited for the door to close, listening to the soft, fading thud of hooves. At last the latch clicked, and the crack of light reappeared at the threshold.

They forced themselves to move slowly until they were well clear of the depot, perspiring with the fear that they had lost the Marmont cash shipment. Suppose, Ki pointed out, Mac had not taken the direction that the sounds had indicated, had doubled back or gone some other way. Once past the town limits, they goaded their horses into a gallop along the wagon road bearing west, toward Orting.

And they nearly overrode their man.

Suddenly, so many things happened so quick that Jessie was never able to put them together in a picture that satisfied her later. Evidently, Mac had heard them coming and had drawn off to the side to see who they were or let them go by. Whatever; he'd backed into the dark, tree-shrouded undergrowth and his grulla stepped on a branch. Thankfully, Ki heard the snap, for Jessie did not. It was the voice she heard first, startled and angry, barking, *"You two!"* The trunk of a pine directly across the road erupted into flying splinters from a heavy gunshot. She rolled sideward in her saddle to protect herself, twisting, reaching for her holstered pistol. She heard Mac's scream then, simultaneously with the *thwack* of a spinning steel *shuriken* burying itself in solid bone. As though in a trance, she glimpsed Mac tumble to the brushy ground, his eyeballs upturned like hard-boiled eggs, the quill vest across his heart jerking erratically as he sucked in his last couple of breaths.

"Damn!" Ki swore, dismounting hastily. "You okay?"

"I'm fine," Jessie answered, shivering. "And if you're cussing because you killed him, don't on my account. I doubt we could've followed a trail-smart killer like Mac all the way back to his boss, or wherever he was to take the cash." She glanced over at the grulla, which was pawing nervously beside its dead rider. "Now it's a matter of what we're going to do with it—"

She was interrupted by a sudden great roar rending the night air. Pausing, she stared off in the direction of Zenobia, then laughed softly as comprehension struck her.

"*That's* what Lysander was 'set' for! Blew up his own safe to make it look like a real robbery."

"Yeah, and we better be getting out of here," Ki said, catching up the reins of the grulla. "It could get nasty for us to be caught with the loot out of that safe."

Swiftly, Jessie transferred the two manila envelopes to her saddlebags and started westward without waiting for Ki. He, meanwhile, dumped Mac cross-saddle on the grulla like a sack of feed, used the man's belt to tie him steady, then tied the grulla's reins to his own saddle and rode on after Jessie. Instead of catching up, he maintained the distance, allowing Jessie to act as a forewarner in case they encountered any other riders.

Their luck held. The storm kept rumbling threateningly but held off, and they reached the relay station at South Prairie without passing a soul. While Ki trotted his horse and the body-laden grulla around to the back clearing, Jessie dismounted in front of the cabin that served as living quarters for the agent. As only a woman can, she set up a door-pounding, general racket enough to raise the dead. It rousted the agent, who wrenched open the door and glared out, wearing a nightcap, sacking nightshirt, and enormous carpet slippers on his skinny feet.

"What crossbred, caterwaulin' idjit—" Ethel fell back, astonished. "Why—why, Miz Starbuck! What'n Tophet did—"

"Quiet!" Jessie cautioned, brushing past him. "We've come from Zenobia, Ethel." She paused as Ki hurried in, closing the door behind them and handing the two manila envelopes to Ethel, who looked at them perplexedly. Jessie told him, "Get some clothes on and make us some coffee, will you? We'll explain."

Soon the three were seated around a rickety table. Jessie filled Ethel in on what had happened, then said, "There aren't too many men in this world I'd bank on, Ethel, but you're one of them."

The agent seemed to puff up from the compliment, his fish eyes taking on a fresh sparkle. "So if I understand you, that toad Lysander is involved in this to some extent or another, likely a lot of extent." He sat a moment in thought, then said slowly, looking at the envelopes, "Lysander got that job at Zenobia about eight months ago. And I happen to know that Fitzpatrick helped him get the appointment."

"*Hugh* Fitzpatrick, of Fitzpatrick and Locke, the trading-post owners?"

"Yup. Always acts like a nice-enough feller when he stops by now'n then, despite his reputation. Oh, it was just a flash guess. He's likely okay."

Jessie nodded noncommittally, then changed topics. "I remember overhearing Mr. Marmont saying he was sending this cash for a heavy equipment order. By any chance, would you know what company that might be?"

"Well, like all the other loggers in these parts, Marmont deals almost exclusively with a jobber in Tacoma, name of Pacific-Cascade Machine and Tool. They always quote the best prices, in turn for cash payment in full before shipping. Betcha Marmont's dealing with 'em."

"All right, Ki will address the envelopes to Pacific-Cascade, in block print so nobody will be able to identify the handwriting," Jessie said. "Then you send them out by the next stage."

"But how're we gonna explain things?" Ethel demanded. "All of Zenobia must know by this time that Lysander's been robbed, and the news'll spread."

"Easy," Jessie told him. "You found the envelopes, all addressed, on your doorstep this morning. You don't know how they got there, but you sent them on as usual, before you'd heard about any robbery at the Zenobia depot."

"But—"

"No buts," Jessie insisted. "Folks'll come to think that the robber got cold feet and decided to turn good, or they won't. Either way, the robber will appear to've disappeared, hightailing it for other pastures."

Ki spoke up. "If you've got a shovel, and an out-of-the-way spot where a dig won't be spotted, I'll set to work making Mac disappear. Oh, yes—and have you means to make his horse and gear vanish, too?"

"I reckon," Ethel admitted reluctantly. "I dunno . . ."

"Please, you must do this! Flaming Geyser is hanging on by a thread, and we're not even smelling on the right trail yet. If whoever's trying to ruin Quinn Abbott get a whiff that anyone's after them, they'll shut down tight and we won't find out a thing."

That seemed to convince Ethel. "Very well, Miz Starbuck, I'm with you. For the future of Mist' Abbott an' Flaming Geyser, I'm with you all the way."

★

Chapter 8

Come morning, the storm had tapered off and the day began cloudy but dry. Jessie and Ki, leaving the Neskowin Inn to get breakfast, acted appropriately shocked upon hearing of the bodacious safecracking at the Flaming Geyser depot. For a few minutes, they joined the handful of loafers still standing about gawking at the building's blown-out door and windows. They learned that Deputy Sheriff Maxwell had already inspected the damage, having returned to town shortly after dawn, and that at the moment he was ensconced in his office with an indignant Sherwin Lysander and a bevy of irate townsfolk. This was not the time, Jessie decided, to drop in on him for a chat.

For the balance of the morning, they played matchstick poker under some trees that bordered the wagon road at the west edge of town. They stayed there, keeping an eye on the road, until a bit after one in the afternoon, when the Starbuck Seattle field agent, Valentine Gresham, appeared driving eleven head of tired horses. He passed them without so much as a twitch of an eyebrow in recognition, moving on toward the livery stable where, according to Jessie's telegraphed instructions, he was to put up the horses in the corral. And in the process, he was to inform the hostler and everyone else he could collar that he was rarin' to sell his weary stock.

Jessie and Ki made a point of being in the Neskowin Inn lobby, lounging in chairs, when Gresham arrived from his business at the livery. He was a man on the cusp of thirty, too young for the lines that were stamped at the corners of his mouth, or for the narrowed hardness of his eyes. With sandy sun-bleached hair and an aquiline nose, he was so lean he seemed dehydrated, and had a sinuous, Indian-bow resilience to his movements. As caked with dust and sweat as his horses, he wore ragged denims like some lowdown scummy forest-rat, except for one detail—his gunbelt, holster, and Smith & Wesson .44 revolver were mighty well cared for.

At the lobby counter, Gresham declared "T. T. Ophir," as he swung the register around to sign. "Need a room and bath privileges."

The clerk looked him up and he looked him down. "There's a water trough around the corner on the main street." He sniffed. "If you bathe here, I'll have to bury the tub afterwards."

Gresham shrugged. "Your choice."

"Choice?"

"Just what gets buried," Gresham said meaningfully.

The clerk paled. "Room Fourteen, bath at the end of the hall."

Gresham stomped upstairs with his key. A few minutes later, Jessie and Ki strolled up as though going to their rooms, but after making sure they were alone, they knocked on Gresham's door. The field agent let them in and locked the door behind them.

"I ain't smelled worse," Gresham complained, "since I peered into a log and caught the south end of a north-pointing skunk. And my name!"

Jessie smiled. "Why, I think T. T. Ophir is rather distinguished. Especially for a horse trader of questionable stock."

"Nothing questionable about them, Miz Starbuck. I scoured Seattle for them Conestoga horses, and I warrant they're the best available, direct descendants of Flemish stallions and Virginia mares."

"I don't mean their bloodlines; I mean their ownership, Val. And I really appreciate how quick you were in following through, buying them and driving them here without explanation."

"Well?" he urged, hoping for an explanation now.

"Well, you just keep on as T. T. Ophir, horse trader."

"Whatever you say; you're the boss. But I'll be darned if I see the sense in bringing such an expensive breed—why, you've got two grand tied up in them Conestogas—with the chance of their being lifted right out from under our noses."

"What makes you think that?" Jessie asked innocently.

"Because there's plenty of quick getaways into the hills from that corral. It's poorly fenced and as wide open as a sieve. Looks like a senseless risk to me."

"Well, Val, that's the reason I had to bring those horses here. I hope somebody *does* steal them, and I hope he does it darned quick."

Flabbergasted, Gresham stared at her.

"Trust me, Val. It's a shot in the dark, but I'm hoping to hit something."

"As you say, Miz Starbuck. I'm gonna bunk down close to the corral, anyway."

"Not tonight. You hit the bars, brag up your stock, show them to whoever's interested. We'll watch tonight. You get a good rest; you look like you need it." Jessie opened the door to go, then paused to add, "Oh, yes, and if any of the horses are missing tomorrow, just sit tight. Tell anybody who asks that they must've strayed."

Gresham sighed the sigh of men plagued by women.

On the way downstairs to the lobby, Jessie remarked to Ki, "Let's see if the sheriff is free now. I mean to have a word with him before the afternoon is over."

As it turned out, the sheriff was free—if not wildly exuberant over visitation by still more citizenry. They found him slumped at his desk in a small, square office, whose walls were tacked with dodger posters and a calendar from a seedhouse showing a golden cornucopia spilling out such big garden vegetables they were scary. He was wearily rubbing the back of his withered neck with liniment. In the aftermath of the safecracking, he seemed more than ever a man of troubles and ailments, trials and tribulations.

"Take a chair," he said unenthusiastically.

"Thanks, but no," Jessie replied. "We won't be here that long."

"Glory be. Well, what's your pleasure? Last night's thievery and destruction? Somebody or somebodies unknown blasted a hole through the depot's safe—an Acme Fireproof Business—that peeled the five-flange door open like a banana. Blew the office out with it, and the waiting room's in kindling."

"My question has to do with the raids on the logging camps."

"Ah, well, I can't even answer where the county's gonna get the money for coffins. That's where I was yesterday, up negotiating with Hugh Fitzpatrick for a bulk price on pine boxes to crate all those dead raiders. Two wagons stacked with 'em! Ain't there no more decency and respect for moderation? At this rate, our Boot Hill's gonna have a bigger population than the town."

"No, what I'm wondering is if you see any pattern to how the camps are raided—if they generally all get hit at the same time."

"Yeah, come to think of it. Seems if one gets hit heavy, the rest get their share."

"And when do the raids happen?"

Maxwell looked puzzled a moment, then said, "Why, most any time the devils take a mind to pull 'em, I reckon."

"You mean there hasn't been anything unusual happening around Zenobia, around this area, just before or after the raids?"

"No," Maxwell replied slowly after thinking over the question. "Ain't been a thing outta the ordinary. What're you driving at, anyhow?"

"I'm not sure. It just strikes me odd that the camps get raided but nothing is stolen—just gangs of gunmen shooting off all night, then riding off just before dawn."

"Men are killed," Maxwell said.

"True, but that can't be the reason for the raids. No, from what you and Rod Delmonico tell me, the raiders hit one camp hard and the others with just enough men to keep them sitting tight and dodging bullets. It's as though they don't want the loggers helping one another on those particular nights."

"But why?" Maxwell demanded. "Owlhoots don't do nothin' unless there's loot in it. Apparently, these raids don't gain them a thing, and that's all wrong. So what're they up to?"

Ki spoke up then. "Catch some of them alive, and maybe they'll tell you before you hang them. That'd make you satisfied, wouldn't it?"

"It would make me satisfied to catch them, young man, but I doubt if I'd hang them. Unless they talked impudent to me, like you're doing."

Ki grinned. "Excuse me."

Maxwell nodded. "Excuse acknowledged and accepted."

"Trouble with me," Ki said, "I got into the habit of hard-talking around campfires and cook-wagons."

"Then you're lucky you lived so long," Maxwell retorted. "Them sort of environs is where I got into the habit of easy-talking."

"Well, I'm through with my talking," Jessie said. "For now. Thank you, Sheriff." She started for the door, Ki falling in alongside her.

Maxwell put the liniment bottle on the desktop and said, "I don't suppose you ever need liniment; you're too young and healthy. But if you ever do, try some of this. I make it myself. It's so pure you could almost drink it. All you need is alcohol, cayenne pepper, and turpentine."

"I'll keep it in mind," Jessie replied, repressing a shudder.

Jessie saw the sheriff again that afternoon, when she attended the ad hoc coroner's jury he had to hold for legal proprieties. Officially finding the dead raiders deceased through self-defense took less time than it did to gather the jurors, and at that, the only reason the twelve men got together was that the meeting was convened in the Neskowin Inn barroom and each juror was guaranteed a free drink. This allowed Jessie, seated in the dining room, to eye comings and goings and to hear the latest rumor-mongering, while keeping to the strictures of proper ladylike decorum.

Ki, meanwhile, took to loafing on a sidewalk bench across from the livery's corral. He used it more or less as a bed, apparently dozing on his side, his hands under his head, his ankles hanging over its end. Through slitted lids he watched whoever came by to look over the horses "T. T. Ophir" was selling. Over the course of the afternoon, a number of potential buyers and onlookers appeared, some of them hanging around the corral or returning a second time. Somewhat to Ki's surprise, though, none was Sherwin Lysander, who by all logic should've been keenly interested. The horses, being Conestogas, weighed a good eighteen hundred pounds each, averaged sixteen hands high, and in teams could lug big, fully loaded freight wagons twelve to eighteen miles a day. They were precisely the breed Flaming Geyser needed to replace the stock lost from the fire. But the agent did not show.

One gent, though, caught Ki's attention by the length of time he stayed. That, and the fact he stuck strictly to himself, and studied each horse with thorough and separate attention. There was one other factor: The man, gaunt, with filmy eyes, wore tight leather brush protectors over his grubby denim pants. At first glance, he looked to Ki like an ordinary down-at-the-heels saddle tramp. A saddle tramp in log country seemed peculiar enough, but one inspecting horses to buy was so out of place that Ki made a closer inspection. A sixth sense, a kind of gut intuition, told him that the man was more than a tramp, that he somehow lived on some kind of third-rate gunplay. For the time being, Ki put him down as a robber, on dark nights, of old men, women, and children.

At sundown, after potential buyers had ceased coming around, Ki ambled across to the stable and asked the hostler if he knew the man. The hostler hemmed a bit, but, plied with four bits, recollected he'd seen the rascal around now and then and understood he was an itinerant odd-jobber answering to the name of Teat. That was all.

Later, over supper, Ki told Jessie about the man Teat. Initially, she was more intrigued by Lysander not appearing, hating to abandon the trail of him, for she was convinced after the previous night's phony burglary that the agent would never be satisfied with making an honest living. In other words, that there was a good chance of his being mixed up with any horse stealing that might occur. But Teat, at the present, seemed the better bet.

In one respect, however, it didn't matter. Lysander, Teat, St. Nick, and a troupe of fairy elves—whoever might show up at the corral—Jessie and Ki would be ready for them. Just as they had the previous night, they saddled up and left the livery as though riding off somewhere, only to covertly double back and tie their horses some fifty yards away from the corral. And, like before, the night blackened with an overcast sky, shrouding them in deep shadow as they silently watched . . . and waited . . .

All remained calm. . . .

It was eerie, holding still, keeping alert as the hours dragged by. The tense night continued. No trouble. Jessie grew irritated with herself, but she stayed with it, even after she became certain she must've been wrong . . .

Eventually, after an eternity, Zenobia lay hushed in the predawn stillness between three and five A.M., when sleep is soundest and those yet awake are at their most relaxed. Most of the Conestogas were lying down, still so tired from the grueling drive from Seattle that they stirred only slowly when a man appeared in the darkness among them.

"Surprise, surprise," Ki whispered. "It's Teat."

The man acted as though he knew exactly what horses he wanted. He chose the five out of the eleven that had been broken to lead, roped them together, head to tail, and left them standing while he quietly lowered the crosspoles in a section of the corral fence. Then, getting his saddle horse, Teat led the Conestogas out, put the section back together, mounted, and rode slowly and almost noiselessly out of the sleeping town, heading west.

Jessie and Ki followed, keeping just in hearing of the horses ahead. Unlike the previous night, they were determined not to let their quarry suspect pursuit until he arrived at wherever he was going. Of course, this could've been Teat's own private thievery and have nothing to do with the systemized banditry directed against Flaming Geyser.

They passed the spot where Mac had died, and continued on for about another mile. Abruptly, Teat and the horses vanished from the wagon road. It took Jessie and Ki precious minutes to discover where Teat had cut off to the right on a little-used, brush-concealed game track.

"At a guess," Jessie remarked as they pushed through the brush, "I'd say this's where Mac would've turned off last night."

The path burrowed through the bordering woods in a northerly course, but it was hard to tell for sure, and grew increasingly harder. They had followed some twisted trails in their time, but this one had all others topped. They knew they must be heading into the Delmonico timberlands, and that the tract couldn't run for more than four or five miles before hitting the White River, yet they followed Teat's path all the rest of the night, up hill and down, into gorges and out of them, and across creeks until they were completely lost.

As dawn broke, they were forced to drop back, keeping to the screening of trees and boulders. At daylight, they were able to follow by track instead of by sound. Every so often, they would run across an intersection of paths, and on more than one occasion they had to stop at forks and crossings for Ki to read which way Teat was leading the horses. This became a little easier as morning eased to noon with a light sprinkling of rain, making fresh imprints more noticeable. Yet there was a tenseness to the cooling drizzle, a hush as if the hills resented their intrusion, and the thickening flurry of clouds; it made them extra-watchful and on edge as they snaked their way through blanketing timber, fissured escarpments, and clefted, rock-strewn culverts.

Eventually, rounding the base of a beetling bulge of a hill, they saw that the path ascended a gentle slope toward an aspen-crowned ridge. And Ki, sniffing the air, halted and lifted his hand.

"Smell anything?" he asked Jessie.

"Smoke," she promptly replied. "Either Teat's taking a cook-break, or we've found his destination."

"Let's take it slowly," Ki advised.

"Yes, sneaky does it." Jessie edged her mare off-trail, Ki following, and they eased their way toward the slope. Soon they came upon a little open glade, where they dismounted and ground-tied their horses. Unsheathing their saddle carbines, they cautiously hiked up the slope and entered a tangle of shrubs and trees near the rim. They stood in the shade there for a while, listening for Teat or other men, looking for a telltale ribbon of smoke. Then, moving to their left, they struggled through a cluttered stand of conifers, eventually emerging where a rotted tree had settled, roots upended, by the very edge of a rimrock.

Crouching there, they stared over the edge and saw a gravelly hillside that sloped gradually for some thirty or forty feet to a rubble-strewn basin. In the slope directly opposite them was a narrow gap—obviously the main entrance to the basin—and not far from it was the dark maw of a mine entrance. Adjacent to the mine was a squat, crudely built shaft house, with mounds of mine tailings and a shack for a rock crusher and sluice pump along one side. On the other side were several ore wagons, a string of tool sheds ending with a tiny lean-to of scrap lumber, and finally a roped-off horse corral over in a patch of weeds and spindly trees.

Even at a distance, Jessie and Ki could readily identify the five footsore Conestogas dwarfing the other horses in the corral. The man huddled in the lean-to was harder to recognize; but what was clear was that he was gaunt and shackled to the lean-to by a short length of chain. He was far from the only man in the basin, however, although the almost three dozen others in view were vastly different—cold-eyed, hard-faced buckos, of the sort that fought only in packs and against what they considered weaker men. Six or so were gathered at a fire, cooking something in a cast-iron kettle. Most were around the mine and shaft house, some carrying full, obviously heavy gunnysacks to men who were stacking the sacks in the wagons, while others simply lounged about, smoking cigarettes and watching. The rest appeared unorganized and undisciplined, which didn't surprise Jessie. And whatever else they were, they were not defense-conscious. The surrounding hills evidently were assumed to provide sufficient protection. They were in a natural pocket with only one gap, after all, requiring only one shot by a lookout to warn them of an attack.

Thoughtfully, Jessie and Ki scanned a bit longer, then slipped into the brush and hiked back to the spot where they'd begun their climb. Descending, they hurried to return the way they'd come, still keeping a cautious eye on the surrounding terrain.

They had backtracked perhaps a quarter of the distance to the wagon road when they crested a hill and glimpsed a man riding toward them. The figure rode furtively, studying the growth on either side, hesitating from time to time to peer and listen. They eased their horses into a shouldering fringe of huckleberry and young oak until they were concealed from the path. Senses acute, they waited.

Presently, the click of hooves came, and through the foliage they watched the rider's approach. After another moment they exchanged grins, recognizing Sheriff Maxwell. They remained hidden, though, while the lawman crested the hill, paused to glance about, then rode on slowly, apparently satisfied. Not until Maxwell was past them did Jessie call to him, a note of amusement in her voice.

"You're on the right track, Sheriff!"

Maxwell whirled in his saddle, his hand pawing for his revolver. Then abruptly his hand dropped and he gave an unamused grunt, as Jessie and Ki emerged casually from the brush.

"What brings you by?" Ki asked conversationally.

"Perhaps I wanted to tell you to tighten up your rein a little."

"Just a friendly warning, eh?"

"Not especially friendly," the sheriff said mildly. "Then again, perhaps I wanted to take advantage of your foolhardy manner, and took to following you." He hesitated expectantly, but when they didn't respond, he went on. "That horse-tradin'

T. T. Ophir character and you, Ki, bench-snoozin' all afternoon was too much to swallow as coincidental. So I went to the livery stable and filed big notches in your horses' shoes. At first light this morning, soon's I saw that some of them horses got lifted, I began bird-dogging your tracks. Wouldn't have done it if I'd knowed what else to do, but I've been combing these hills for months and've gotten precisely nowhere."

"You may have this time, and you certainly saved us a trip hunting you up," Jessie replied, her smile widening. "It never occurred to me that we might be followed. Sure is one on us, Sheriff, but now we'd better move before somebody back behind us fancies to ride this way."

The three proceeded toward the wagon road at a gentle lope. Jessie told the sheriff of tracing the horses and their thief to the basin, and briefly sketched the situation and her suspicions. "My sense is that the encampment is on Delmonico land, all of half a mile from the White River," she said. "But what a weary way we had to come to reach it! That roundabout chase was solely for the purpose of shaking off any possible pursuit. Such secrecy, in fact, is the reason behind most, possibly all, of the goings-on. Clearly, this gang has been keeping the loggers holed up in their own camps, nailed down tight defending their homes and property, in order to haul some sort of secret cargo at night without anyone the wiser."

"And you say they're operatin' a mine?"

"Yes, but mining what, I can't tell. I mean, it has all the earmarks of coal—"

"Coal!" Maxwell blurted. "King County has a few deposits, but I never heard tell of any here in Pierce. Besides, even if there were, coal ain't worth diddly-squat."

"I agree; coal certainly isn't valuable enough for all the trouble and bloodshed. I imagine we won't know for sure what they're digging up and freighting out until we take the basin. Or unless we make Fitzpatrick and Locke confess."

"The trading-post owners? You think they're mixed in this?"

"They have to be, Sheriff. The basin is near a river in a remote, unlogged corner of Delmonico property, precisely the area where trappers would still be working—and where Fitzpatrick and Locke would be trading, privy to everything that's happening. And what *is* happening? Trappers are getting rousted, shot up, held at bay as much as the loggers. Like you yourself said, both sides are busy accusing the other of skullduggery, and might well be wrong. And they are. They've been tricked into feuding, which serves as a smoke screen to prevent detection of the basin and the shipments. No, Fitzpatrick and Locke must surely be aware, perhaps bought off or deeply involved, just as greed must've gotten the better of Sherwin Lysander."

"Well, that verminous threesome are in for a fall when they learn of the raidings and killings they've become party to." Maxwell's cheeks reddened with ire. "Soon's I get to town, I'm organizing everyone from everywhere into the biggest damn posse, and then I'm going to go clean out that basin!"

Jessie shook her head. "Don't risk a posse. It'd take too much time to form and would probably tip off the gang. Moreover, charging in there would surely result in Dion Nettle being killed."

"That was Nettle they're holding prisoner?"

"Nobody else is reported missing. Whoever the man is, though, we ought to try to rescue him. I suggest we go gather some of the Delmonico crew. They'll be pleased to get in some licks, and I know they can be trusted. They'll be all the posse we'll need."

"What, agin a mob of gunmen?" The sheriff balked. "We'd have as much chance as a rabbit in a hound dog's mouth."

"I think we'd have a good chance. Judging by the way they were loading the wagons, chances are they're planning to ship out tonight. That means most of the gang'll be off raiding logging camps and maybe trapper digs, too."

"Then we've got to warn—"

"We can't, Sheriff," Jessie insisted. "The camps took care of themselves before, and we simply have to count on them putting up a good scrap again. It's the only way that'll allow us to attack so swiftly and surprisingly that those remaining in the basin will be caught off-guard, and won't have a chance to mount a defense." She mulled this over for a moment, then added with a frown, "Even so, it could easily turn into a fight to the death, no quarter given."

★

Chapter 9

By the time Jessie, Ki, and Maxwell reached the Delmonico camp, it was late afternoon, almost dusk. The sky had turned overcast again with slate-gray clouds, and a breeze was beginning to whip up, swirling bits of grit and fallen leaves in eddies before it. But upon riding into the yard, they saw the main cabin cheerily aglow with lamplight and could hear a fiddler inside ripping through a spritely version of "Camptown Races."

"Now what?" Ki said, then grinned. "Opal's birthday party!"

Jessie brightened. "Good, we arrived just in time."

"And me with her present back in my office," Maxwell grumphed.

"We give Dion Nettle to her alive and in one piece," Jessie declared, "and unless I miss my guess, that's all the present Opal will fancy."

At the stable, they unsaddled and turned their mounts into the corral, which was already fairly crowded with the horses of the party guests. Jessie, mulling things over as they walked to the cabin, got to the front door and was about to enter when she turned to Ki and the sheriff.

"Listen; I think I've figured out a couple more pieces and how they fit into this puzzle. I can't explain now, not out here. But when we go in, don't say anything."

"Not even happy birthday?"

She cut Ki a look. "I mean about what we've found out. First we must get Rod Delmonico, Sheales, and his man Busch off someplace alone, like in one of the bedrooms where we can shut the door. Then be ready to back up any play I make."

"When we get overwrought," Maxwell said kindly, "sometimes we don't know what we're thinking."

"I never get overwrought!"

"That's fine," Maxwell said. He patted Jessie on the top of the head, as though she were a small boy, knocked politely on the door, and stepped inside.

A fuming Jessie and Ki entered close behind.

The parlor and dining room were noisy with party guests. A haze of cigar smoke mingled with appetizing odors wafting from the kitchen, and once more the dining-room table struggled under the weight of food, laid out buffet-style around a cauldron-sized punchbowl. Rod Delmonico was spooning potato salad onto his plate; Yachats

Sheales and Bender Busch were conversing with three other loggers; and Pierce Thorleigh, uncomfortable in a string tie, was enduring the company of a spinster. The fiddler, on a break, was waggling his violin bow to emphasize some point to Opal Delmonico, who immediately excused herself and hurried over to greet the new arrivals.

Jessie and Ki spent the next twenty minutes in introductions and chitchat, Opal shepherding them from guest to guest. Eventually, though, they broke away and, aided by the sheriff, maneuvered Rod and Sheales into a private meeting in Jessie's guest bedroom. Bender Busch accompanied his boss, and apparently that was reason enough for Pierce Thorleigh to tag along as well.

"Now, what's so all-fired important that we gotta sneak ourselves off from the party?" Rod demanded once they were in the room. "Maxwell? Is this some notion of yours?"

"Nope." The sheriff leaned back against the closed door. "I believe Miz Starbuck is superintendin' this session. Me, I'm just along to make sure she don't pull no female wiles that'll trance us to act unsocial."

Sheales began, "What's that supposed to mean—"

"*Mister* Sheales," Jessie interrupted sharply, "when we first met a few days ago, only you, the Delmonicos, Ki, and myself knew that Ki would be going to that clearing by Cedar Creek. And you alone had the opportunity to pass on that information to the raiders so they could ambush him."

"A coincidence—"

"They were waiting for Ki and called him by name!"

"This's preposterous!" Sheales retorted. "Raiders have shot up my camps and hurt my men same as they have other loggers."

Ki responded, "A cover-up. That old game has whiskers." He took a step toward Sheales. "Maybe you don't head the raiders, but you're definitely in cohoots with them. It's all up, Sheales; admit it!"

Sheales gulped thickly, said nothing.

"Yachats," Rod demanded, his face a portrait of shock. "Yachats, is this true?"

Instead of Sheales, Busch answered. "Naw, of course it ain't true! These two strangers come stickin' their noses into our affairs, and when they can't find out who's behind the outlawry, they try to pin the blame on somebody—anybody! They oughtta be horsewhipped!"

"Horsewhippin' sounds powerful unsociable to me," Maxwell commented, drawing his revolver. He held it casually at his side, not threateningly, not yet. "So happens these strangers located the bandit hideout. Soon's we clean out that nest, we'll have plenty of testifiers to the factuals, and if they don't want to talk to keep from hanging, they've got a gent prisoner there I warrant will be glad to bear witness—Dion Nettle."

"He's one of the killers hisself!" Busch accused hotly. "Everybody knows about him turnin' bad and disappearin' with the Delmonico payroll."

"Dion, no, he—" Thorleigh blurted, part a gasp, part a groan. Then, when the others glanced sharply at him, he stiffened, his face paling. "I . . . Mist' Delmonico, I gotta confess something. Y'know there's been talk of information leakin' out of camp. Well—I'm the spy."

"What?" Rod bellowed. "What kinda yarn are you tryin' to spin?"

"It's the truth. After Nettle disappeared, I was as puzzled as anybody. I couldn't believe that he'd turned bad." Thorleigh paused, then rushed on, "Well, y'know how I hang my coat on a peg on the corral fence by the well when I'm workin' around there. One day, I found a letter in a pocket. It flabbergasted me. I've got it for you to see. One sheet was from Dion Nettle, no mistakin' his scrawl, and it said, 'They've got me a prisoner in their hideout camp, Pierce. There's no joke about this.' "

"Prison camp!" Rod exclaimed.

"Yeah. It must be the place Miz Starbuck an' Ki found. That's why I'm confessin', now we know where Nettle is, on account the second note said that if I didn't do what was wanted, they'd kill him. The note ordered me to meet somebody on the trail between here and Mist' Sheales's camp."

"Did you go?" Rod asked.

"Yeah. That night. I was met by two men, one who did the talkin' while the other held a gun on me. He told me I was to let 'em know everything—if you sent for help, or made any move against the raiders. I was to put a note under a certain rock by the trail, and they was to leave my orders there. I thought about puttin' some of the boys in hidin' and catchin' them, but that've meant Nettle's death. So I . . . I decided to trail along till I found out what they wanted, till I could think of some plan to beat 'em at their game."

"There's your snitch!" Bender Busch snapped. "Mist' Sheales is due an apology, and don't figure that'll make amends, neither—"

"But I didn't know that Ki was goin' to Cedar Creek," Thorleigh objected. "I didn't know nothing about that till he got back, and we went to get the bodies. I recognized two of 'em as the pair I met o'er by Sheales's camp, so for Nettle's safety, I rode over and left a message about it." He pointed an accusing finger at Busch and Sheales. "I always wondered who'd had a chance to slip that original letter into my pocket. Well, now it occurs to me that the only visitors we had here that day was you, Busch, and you, Mist' Sheales. You must've seen me hangin' my coat on the peg when you were watering your horses at the well trough. One of you must've put the letter in my pocket."

"Why, cuss yuh!" Busch snarled, lunging at Thorleigh.

Maxwell stopped him, poking the gun muzzle hard into his ribs. "Whoa up, there. You ain't bein' sociable a'tall."

"He's lyin'!"

"Oh, what's the use?" Sheales groaned, slumping on the edge of the bed. "They know everything, or soon will f'sure."

"You admit it, then?" Rod charged.

"I . . . I knew all about it," Sheales replied. "I countenanced it. I couldn't do anything else. Like

Thorleigh here, they had me in a bind."

"Do some quick talking!"

"Well, Rod, everything seemed to go wrong after my wife died. I got deeper into debt, down to not bein' able to meet payroll. Then Bender Busch showed me a way out."

"Keep your cussed mouth shut!" Bender warned.

Maxwell prodded with his gun. "Keep your'n shut."

"Busch had friends with a lot of money, he told me," Sheales continued doggedly. "His pals turned out to be Fitzpatrick, Locke, and that infernal Sherwin Lysander. They bought up my notes from the bank in Tacoma and made me a new long-term loan. I was thankin' 'em for it when I learned the truth."

"Which was?" Rod demanded.

"Busch was to run my outfit, and they was to work a scheme to keep the other loggers down and out of the way while they concentrated on ruinin' you. I don't know why, they never confided in me, but they had some source of money and promised me a share so's in time I could buy up my notes. I . . . I was too weak to resist, I reckon. So I let 'em have their way."

"Why didn't you come to me, Yachats? I'd have helped you get out of the mess."

"Had too much pride, Rod." Sheales shrugged. "You got everything, and I got nothing. I got into this mess almost before I knew it, and I've a hunch Busch helped engineer things agin me. Well, I can't undo what's done, but I can help set things straight. Rod, Sheriff Maxwell, Sherwin

Lysander's got a little black book that's got all the names o' the fellers who're in on this. It tells how much each one's take is." Sheales's voice had grown vindictive, but now he took a deep breath and made a wide gesture with his hands. "Well, that's all. I reckon I'm going to jail, maybe even stretch rope. But I won't go alone, not when you latch onto that black book. And Bender Busch, he'll be going with me—if not before!"

Suddenly, Sheales whipped out a hammerless "Banker's Special" pocket pistol from his coat. Before anyone could stop him, he triggered it point-blank at Busch. Busch caught the first slug in his chest and a second through his heart; he collapsed just as Maxwell, springing forward, cracked his own revolver down on Sheales's head. Sheales fell back, stunned, and lay limply across the bed. Jessie and Ki, meanwhile, knelt by Busch, although there was nothing they could do for the man.

The fiddle music stopped suddenly and there was a babble of excited voices.

Rod Delmonico darted to the door and turned the key in the lock. Somebody knocked. "Rod? What's happened? Is anything wrong?"

"Nothing's wrong, Opal," Rod called hastily to his sister. "Y'all go back and enjoy the party. We were just tryin' out a gun."

As the voices on the other side of the door began to fade, there came a squeak of springs from the bed. What with Busch on the floor and the clamor from outside, nobody had been paying attention to Sheales, who, they'd assumed, was unconscious from the blow on his head. But Sheales was moving, and abruptly another shot reverberated in the room. Sheales still clutched his smoking pistol in his hand; the hole in his temple revealed he had taken the quickest way out.

"Two dead men," Maxwell said somberly. "Miz Opal's shindig or no shindig, Mist' Delmonico, we can't lock no door on this."

Going out to a distressed Opal and her disconcerted guests, Rod and the sheriff, flanked by Jessie, Ki, and Thorleigh, tried to smooth over the tragedy as much as possible. But it had the makings of a scandal, and reaction was that of alarm and horror. The gunfire had also attracted the attention of the jacks around the clearing, and some were running up to the cabin to investigate. These men were pressed into service by Rod, who ordered them to wrap the bodies of Sheales and Busch in blankets and carry them to the stable. There, the sheriff instructed that their horses be saddled and packed with the blanketed bodies for transport to town.

While the bodies were being tied crosswise across the saddles, an extremely upset Rod decided to deal with Pierce Thorleigh. "You, my trusted overseer, connivin' with killers!" he raged. "So it was you who tipped 'em off that Miz Starbuck and Ki were coming?"

"Yeah," Thorleigh said humbly.

"And almost got them killed at that pass!"

"It was either them or Dion Nettle, Mist' Delmonico, and I judged they could take care of themselves. If I hadn't warned the gang, they'd have found out and killed Nettle, maybe. It was Miz Opal I was thinkin' of. If he'd been dead and I'd been the cause—you can see how it was. Maybe I should've come straight to you, but I was afraid that Miz Opal—"

"I oughtta have Maxwell sling your butt into prison, you murderin' lobo!" Rod shouted. "Aidin' and abettin' scoundrelly raiders! You're done on the Delmonico crew, Thorleigh! Roll up your blankets and ride!"

"Rod!" cried a woman's shocked voice from the stable entrance.

Jessie and the men whirled around. Opal Delmonico, ashen-faced, was standing in the entryway, looking at Thorleigh searchingly.

"I overheard it all," she said. "Thanks for what you did, Pierce."

"You thankin' him?" her brother bellowed.

"Don't you understand, Rod?" she said, choking. "He was saving Dion's life for me. He was doing the best he could under the circumstances. What else could he have done? Please, Rod! I'm half-owner, and I want Pierce to stay on."

Rod Delmonico eyed her and did some thinking as some of his hotheaded anger left him. It was beyond him to refuse his sister any favor. "Oh, very well," he reluctantly agreed. "You can stay on, Thorleigh. But don't forget you're on probation."

"Thanks," Thorleigh said dully.

"Thanks are sorely in order," Maxwell told Thorleigh. "Mister Delmonico ain't pressin' charges, so

I ain't arresting you. Whether I'd like to is something else again."

"I'll make it up, I swear. Just give me a chance."

Pierce Thorleigh was almost a wreck, Jessie saw. She reached the decision that the man could be trusted. "You'll have your chance tonight. Have you about a dozen jacks who are good fighters, men you know are loyal?"

"More'n twelve," Thorleigh promptly declared.

"Then this's what I'd like you to do, Pierce. Select your best; have them heavily armed with plenty of extra ammunition, ready to saddle up about ten tonight."

Thorleigh glanced at Rod Delmonico and, catching his boss's nod of approval, declared, "Let's go selectin' right now."

He led the way to the nearest bunkhouse, and as soon as he was inside, he commanded, "Lineup!" Even Rod watched with amazement as the men lined up and Thorleigh began going down the line, picking a man here and there and ordering him to step aside. "Miz Starbuck, I reckon, will be giving you orders," he told the picked men, after explaining they were to be armed and ready by ten. "Any complaints about obeyin' a female?"

"Every man does, sometime or other," one of the men drawled, producing a chorus of laughs.

Then Jessie related how Dion Nettle was imprisoned in the hideout camp of the raiders, and how it was their job to rescue him and end the outlaw scourge. The jacks were all for that, although Jessie declared that more killers might show up at the hidden basin at any time, so there might be more battling than appeared at first.

Just before ten, everyone was gathered outside the stable, horses saddled, weapons cleaned, extra ammunition stuffed into belts and jackets. After the chosen jacks had mounted, Ki turned to Jessie and said, "We've got thirteen, an extra man we didn't bargain for."

"Who?"

"Upwind Muldoon. The old coot says he ain't had any excitement for years, and wants to be in one more ruckus before he dies."

"Oh, for—! Well, we'll keep him back out of harm."

Ki chuckled. "Okay, Jessie. But if his old blood gets to boiling, he'll probably charge right in."

Jessie shook her head, then addressed the group of riders. "Soon as we reach the rim of the basin, get into hiding and keep out of sight."

"What's to wait for?" a jack demanded. "Let's go get 'em!"

"No, you'll likely get killed or shot up and Dion Nettle's life won't be worth a plugged nickel. He has to be brought out, before we attack."

"How're you gonna do that, ma'am?" another jack asked.

"Leave that to me," Ki replied. "While I'm gone, if more raiders show up, be sure your mounts don't nicker. Hold their nostrils, each man to his own horse. If I don't come out with Nettle, if we're trapped, well, then you open up."

"You can save him!" Opal begged anxiously. "I'm sure you can."

"I'll do my best," he said. "Now, do you and Rod think you can hold off a raid with the jacks who're left?"

"Raid?" Rod repeated. "Here again?"

Jessie said, "That's the reason for the raids. They keep you so busy here that you can't wander over your property or travel the wagon roads, Rod, and see what you're not supposed to see."

"You talk in riddles," he complained. "And I hafta say I was expecting to go along with y'all. But I reckon my place is here, with my sister. We'll handle things; don't worry."

"Good," Jessie said. "Let's waste no more time. Come on, Sheriff . . . oh, yes, you're included in this, just to make things all legal."

"Miz Starbuck," Maxwell responded, "I not only make it legal; I make it possible. This's my job, and I should tell you to scat, you bein' a lady too delicate for war-pathin' and liable to suffer from spells o' the vapors and all. But I got a feelin' you'd just follow after us out of sheer contrariness."

Deciding to approach the basin cross-country rather than by the paths the raiders might take, they set off northwesterly from the Delmonico camp. They blazed their own trail, weaving through the night-blurred scrub and rock, clawing along steep slopes and declivities where their horses almost slid on their hindquarters.

Although Maxwell, Thorleigh, and the jacks were far more familiar with the Delmonico terrain, Jessie and Ki scouted as best they could through the roughs of brush, rock, and forest for indications that would lead them back to the bandit hideout.

At one point, Jessie slowed her mare to let the riders pass her, as something off to one side caught her attention for a moment. It was nothing important, she concluded, but then she found a horseman suddenly beside her: Upwind Muldoon.

"Miz Starbuck," Muldoon murmured, "I've got something to tell you when we get a chance and won't be overheard."

"What about?" she asked.

"It ain't foolishness. It's about some man tryin' to kill you from behind."

"Stick beside me," Jessie said in a low voice.

The remainder of the riders passed them, and Jessie and Muldoon gradually let the others get ahead of them a little.

"It's safe enough for you to talk now," Jessie said. "The others are all ahead of us now. What do you know about it, if anything?"

"I know all about it, Miz Starbuck." Muldoon had let his mount close to Jessie's on the left. He did not talk loudly. "I know the man who's after you on account of that Pascal business in Wyoming."

"Who is he?"

"Well, ma'am," Muldoon now said, "I'm the man."

"You?" Jessie turned to stare—

—and at that moment a lariat dropped around her body, pinning her arms to her sides as the noose was drawn taut with a jerk. The next instant, the rope was looped around Upwind Muldoon's saddlehorn, and Jessie felt the muzzle of a pistol boring into her side. The attack had been so unexpected, it caught her off-guard entirely. Of all the men on the Delmonico crew, Jessie would have suspected old Upwind last.

But now suppressed rage filled Muldoon's low voice. "Few folks know it, but Oscar Pascal was my nephew. I was too old to do hard ridin' and hard fightin' with him, but afore he went to Wyoming, I did some of his spyin' and hoss-holdin' for him. Fine boy, he was! And you run him down, and he got killed with the others, them what ain't rottin' in prison!"

Listening to the tirade, Jessie tested the rope that held her arms to her side, but it did not slacken even a trifle. Nor did the pressure of the gun muzzle against her side relax. "If you kill me, Upwind, you'll hang."

"That'll be okay." Muldoon chuckled. "I'm an old man and not worth much anymore. I've been brooding over my nephew ever since I came here. Now I'll handle you, Miz Starbuck, and if I get my chance, I'll handle Ki, too. But Ki's just your Chink lackey, so it's you I'm making sure to get; then they can do what they want with me—if they catch up with me."

"I suppose you're going to shoot me."

"Not lest I hafta," Muldoon said, savoring his revenge. "I've got some bandsaw files with me, long and slender, pointy-ended. If I drive one of 'em into your heart, it'll be a quick finish for you. No noise, either. I'll let you topple out of your saddle, and I'll make a run for it."

"So you have it all planned?" Unable to reach her pistol, much less draw it from her holster,

Jessie tried to work her hand to her belt buckle, praying she could stall him long enough to gain the twin-shot derringer concealed there. But even if she did, it would be perilously difficult to use it before Muldoon blasted her. "What good will it do you to kill me?"

"Be squarin' accounts for Oscar," he growled ominously. Then he laughed. "Think of you comin' to the Delmonicos! Playin' right into my hands."

Jessie jabbed slightly with her right spur, and her mare bumped against Muldoon's horse. That slackened the rope a bit, and as Muldoon worked at his reins to separate the horses so the rope would grow taut again, his gun ceased pressing into Jessie for an instant.

Jessie took a chance then, knowing full well that she was dealing with a desperate, cruel, and quite possibly insane killer. She thrust her arms wide violently, and the noose was loosened enough for her to snag the derringer from behind her buckle. Though she could lift her arm only partway, she fired a wild shot, then yanked her mount back on its haunches.

Upwind Muldoon's howl of rage rang through the night. His pistol blazed and cracked, and the bullet scorched the front of Jessie's blouse, almost shearing off a nipple. She felt the tip of the bandsaw file scratch along her back as Muldoon tried to thrust, which the milling horses wrecked. Yells from up front and the sound of hoofbeats told her help was coming. Before Muldoon could fire again, she managed to twist in her saddle and fire the second shot from her derringer.

With a croaky screech, Muldoon reeled in his saddle. Jessie managed to get outside the noose, and grabbed Muldoon's hand and twisted the pistol out of it. Muldoon struck viciously with the file he still clutched in his left hand, but missed. Then Jessie had her arms around Muldoon and was holding him helpless as Ki, Thorleigh, and the other jacks came charging up.

"Upwind tried to kill me!" Jessie explained, panting. "He's an old-time outlaw and killer, and just now went berserk. Tie him up and keep him in his saddle."

But Muldoon was in a frenzy. He tried to wheel his mount as Jessie let go of him, struck wildly with the file, and ripped Thorleigh's coat sleeve.

"Watch out for him!" Jessie warned.

As Thorleigh and Ki closed in, Muldoon's horse reared and almost fell. The vicious old man gave another wild howl, abruptly collapsed in his saddle, and would have fallen had not Ki held him. Then an errant gleam of starlight showed the long bandsaw file protruding from his chest. Muldoon had found a victim—himself.

Jessie, looking grimly at the body of the old man who had carried a lifetime of evil in his soul, briefly told the others why the man had tried to kill her. "That was one of the tightest corners I've been in," she admitted. "A man who'd worked himself up to the state Upwind had—you never know what he might do, and I daresay he wouldn't always know what he was doing, either. I imagine he figured this would give him a good opportunity, perhaps his last one, if we were successful, to get me alone and kill me in the dark. Well, a man's crimes catch up with him somehow, sometime . . ." Sighing, she turned away. "Well, tie down his body; he'll have to ride along with us before we can return to the camp. And then let's get going. Our work isn't done, remember."

★

Chapter 10

Midnight was nearing, and the quarter moon was casting meager light through rents in the overcast sky, when the riders reached the path that led to the basin. Turning onto the path, proceeding single file in a slow, quiet walk, they kept eyes and ears open for signs of raiders approaching or posted as lookouts. They passed the spot where Jessie and Ki had left their mounts to climb the slope and continued on as the path made a wide sweep around the entire knoll. Darkness blurred the rugged harshness of the surrounding terrain; the forest itself was swathed in gloom, rising steeply toward the ridgeline in black, corrugated smudges of boulders and timber.

Presently, the path intersected a slightly wider, wheel-rutted trail. The riders began heading along the trail, moving more cautiously than ever. At one point a fast-rippling brook slashed across the trail, switching sides for no apparent reason as it and the trail wound toward the hill.

"I bet this stream," Ki murmured to Jessie, "is the water source for the mine's crusher and sluice pump. We must be getting awful close to the hideout."

They headed on for a bit longer, scrutinizing the terrain for signs of life—life that spelled death. The banks on both sides rose higher and drew narrower, fashioning a cleft of sorts wrapped in gloom, falling steeply away from the hill. The brook burbled and stewed, making an S-curve, tall grasses and saplings sprouting in its bend. The trail curved with the brook, and Ki glimpsed slopes of stone around beyond. He held up his hand as a signal to rein in, and Jessie, Maxwell, and the Delmonico crewmen clustered silently around him.

"That dogleg ahead is the start, I think, of the cut into the hideout. It's a great place to stick a guard, and a lousy place for us to get trapped," Ki whispered. "Let's move off-trail, hide the horses, and hike on foot."

Sliding into the concealing woods, they anchored their horses' reins with rocks and silently crawled up to the rim of the basin.

"The mine," Jessie whispered, peering over.

A great deal of activity was going on in the basin. Campfires were burning brightly, and a large number of men were in and around the corral, saddling up. Maxwell brought out a pair of binoculars and focused them on the milling outlaws below; after a moment he let out a disgusted grunt.

"Fitzpatrick," he declared. "I don't see that weasel Urias Locke anywheres, but another man seems to be boss down there, one I don't recognize."

Asking for the glasses, Jessie looked carefully. Maxwell's "stranger" was burly and wolf-jawed, with an old Whitney shotgun crooked in one arm. "That's Plumas, Quinn Abbott's lieutenant." Handing the glasses to Ki, she added, "So it's like I suspected—there *is* a connection between the logcamp trouble and Flaming Geyser's problems. But exactly how they're linked, I've still to figure."

Shortly the outlaws, mounted and gathered in a group, rode out on the wagon trail through the gap.

"Now the raids will start," Maxwell growled. "That bunch will fan out and strike Gawd knows how many camps tonight. I wish—"

"I know," Jessie murmured. "I wish we could stamp them all out in one fell swoop, too. But let's hope if we cut off the head and some of the body, the rest of this snake will be easy to smash."

A half hour later there was more activity, this time concentrated around the shaft house. Men were hastily loading the last of the big ore-wagons, piling the gunnysacks high in the beds, while other men were hitching up teams of six horses per wagon—including, Ki saw through the glasses, the five Conestogas that Mac had stolen. Soon, with cursing yells and lashing whips, the drivers got the wagons moving and wheeled out the gap with their secretive, tarpaulin-draped cargoes. After they had gone, the basin quieted down some.

But plenty of outlaws remained.

Ki stirred restlessly. "Okay, I'm going in for a look," he said, returning the binoculars to Maxwell. "You guys sneak back to your horses and set tight off-trail a while longer. If possible, I'll go all the way in and free Nettle, but in any case, don't do anything till I get back out. That is, unless you hear gunfire, and then come a-stormin'."

"You heard him, boys," Maxwell said, gazing about sternly. "We've got surprise on our side, and maybe we can corral 'em without firing a shot. Let's hope. But if they start slingin' lead, hit 'em hard with all you've got. Understand?"

A low muttering of agreement answered him.

Reasoning that any lookouts would be posted by the gap, Ki started heading in that direction along the rimrock. The firelight from the basin did not reach high enough to illuminate around the rim, and clouds were sifting in front of the moon again, hampering its frail light.

And yet, because it was so dark, Ki caught a spark winking among the rocks above the gap—a spark no brighter or longer than a firefly's wink or the flare of a match. Dropping to his hands and knees, Ki approached, focusing intently. Shortly, he perceived two vague outlines, easily mistaken for boulders, if they hadn't shifted out of boredom. Ki slithered scarcely an inch at a time, gliding around the back of a boulder with his body flat to the ground. Finally, not a yard from them, he was able to identify the two men, one of whom he recognized as the horse thief named Teat.

" . . . Heard noises down thataway," Teat was saying.

"You're always hearing noises," the other scoffed. "Nobody's come by us on the trail, have they? I see your noises, I'll believe 'em."

"Wouldn't hurt to check, just to be sure," Teat said. He stood up, waiting for his partner to rise. "The stretch will do us good."

Ki killed them.

He straightened and tossed daggers with efficient dispatch, having no intention of making it a contest. He had to silence the men as well as drop them, had to make it a swift execution before they could cry out. Teat was first, because his back was to Ki and he would be harder to hit once he started to turn. The blade sank deep into the base of his neck, passing between the vertebrae, slicing his spinal cord and bringing his thievery to an end without so much as a whimper. The other man had his mouth open wide to yell, but could not because his windpipe was severed, along with his jugular vein, which fountained blood as he toppled over.

Immediately, Ki was on the move again, prowling the rest of the crown for more lookouts, but finding none. He glanced down at the bandit camp, gauging the scene revealed by the blazing fires, then cautiously inched his way down the slope. Arriving at the base, he sprinted across the floor of the basin, crouching low and taking such advantage as he could of what little cover was available. Then, pausing at the rear of the nearest shed, he moved silently behind the line of them to the back of the lean-to where Nettle was kept chained. Finally, easing along one side, he craned to peer inside the lean-to.

Nettle was not there. Ki sat back on his haunches in puzzlement, searching about the basin for some sign of the prisoner. Hulking shadows of men could be seen clustered around campfires, talking, drinking, cleaning their weapons. From one fire drifted the strumming of a guitar. Inside the lean-to was what looked to be a bed of sorts made of flattened fir branches, and a short length of chain ran from one pole of the lean-to to an open wrist shackle. But no Dion Nettle. Ki felt a cold chill ripple up his spine. Had he been too late, had Nettle been killed as threatened . . . ?

Then, abruptly, he heard footsteps. From out of the darkness far to his right, two men headed for the lean-to; one was a bandolier-belted bruiser, who had a hand firmly around the arm of a slumping, staggering Dion Nettle. The outlaw flung Nettle into the lean-to, reeled in the trailing chain and padlocked the wrist shackle, then spat at his prisoner.

"That's the last time you're taking a piss tonight," the outlaw sneered. "I don't care if'n you gotta shit, I ain't traipsin' you nowhere again."

Already, Ki was on the move again. Padding noiselessly while the man was talking, careful not to dislodge a loose stone or snap a brittle twig, he stole to within throwing distance—and threw. His dagger speared the man in the throat, lancing through his larynx. The man's startled shout died stillborn, and even as he was falling, Ki crept out and grabbed his leg, dragging the body back out of sight behind the lean-to.

"Whozzat?" Nettle called weakly. "What's goin' on?"

"Quiet," Ki hissed, searching the fallen man's pockets. "I've come from the Delmonicos. Crawl over here where I can unlock your cuff."

Hearing the rustle of fir branches as Nettle shuffled closer, Ki dug out the padlock key and reached around the side of the lean-to, still keeping himself hidden as much as possible. Nettle placed the padlock into his fingers, then muffled the lock with his other hand as Ki, working by touch, opened the lock and removed it from the shackle. Nettle carefully eased his wrist free and put the shackle down so the links would not clink together, then scuttled around the side of the lean-to. Bewhiskered, emaciated, hollow-eyed, his clothes filthy and torn, the young man looked like the survivor of a shipwreck. But at least he was that, a survivor. And he managed to grin.

"I'll never be able to thank you, mister."

Ki touched his lips to warn Nettle that silence was necessary, then began guiding him away from the lean-to along the line of sheds. They were almost to where they'd have to cross open ground to the base of the slope, when a man rounded the corner of a shed and collided with Ki.

The man was startled, but rebounded instantly; despite the darkness, Ki immediately recognized him as the two-gun kid who'd sided Mac. The two-gun kid recognized Ki in turn, and drew. The kid was fast. He'd been born with the skill, had practiced it diligently, and had the confidence to use it effectively. He also had quick-draw holsters, which practically fed the butts of his revolvers into his palm if he so much as flicked his wrists.

He fired twice, once with each revolver. But the second shot was pure reflex; he was already dead. Both shots sailed off harmlessly into the sky as he went over backward with the handle of Ki's slim *tanto* blade protruding from the flesh beneath his chin. Ki had been just a bit faster, stepping forward just as the kid drew, sliding out his knife from his waistline, bringing the point of the blade upward with savage force, plunging it through muscle, tendon, and bone. As the kid hit the ground, Ki moved in. Placing a foot squarely in the kid's face for leverage, he pulled out the blade. Dion Nettle leaned forward and puked.

"So much for getting out the simple way," Ki muttered, snatching Nettle by the arm. They headed across the open ground in a crouching run, and managed to reach the slope before the basin erupted in alarm. Lunging up the slope, they made a third of the distance before the first shot came. It clipped Nettle's tattered shirt, and he shied, looking back over his shoulder, only to trip and sprawl forward. The fall saved his life, for a veritable hail of gunfire swept above them as Ki also dropped to hug the rocks. Then Nettle got to his feet and, with Ki alongside, climbed the slope in a low-hunkering scramble, more rifle and pistol fire chasing them, ricocheting off surrounding stone and splintering woody growth. Coming to a narrow crevice that angled into to the face of the slope like a wedge, they dove into its concealing pocket and—

—and all hell broke loose below.

Spurring in a hard gallop, Sheriff Maxwell and the Delmonico crewmen swept around the dogleg curve and streamed on through the narrow gap. Before the outlaws realized what was going on, the speeding riders were surging into the basin, pouring volleys of fire ahead of them. The next second, the outlaws were scattering afield, whipping up weapons and blasting indiscriminately as they ran for cover. The Delmonico crew, headed by Pierce Thorleigh, plunged forward in pursuit like an avenging tidal wave.

"Surrender!" Maxwell bellowed. "Give up in the name o' the law!"

Instead, the vicious outlaws, fearing the noose, raced for cover behind boulders or into copses, or dodged about in desperate attempts to escape through the gap. The determined crew charged to stop them, their onslaught turning the basin into an inferno of pounding hooves, rearing horses, and blazing guns. Repeatedly, the outlaws were repulsed, thrown back or shot down, yet repeatedly they rallied in frenzied efforts to burst out of this ring of death, firing a deadly response to the crew's challenge.

Yet the end was inevitable. Gradually, gunfire from the outlaws lessened, as their weapons emptied and their numbers dwindled. They fought on like the cornered rats they were, the attack becoming a close-quarter melee of knives and hand-to-hand struggles, but the diminishing survivors could withstand just so much punishment. Sheriff Maxwell's continuing call for surrender began to take effect, and a growing number of outlaws dropped their weapons and raised their hands. Only those off to the sides with any chance to make it sought to flee by scrambling, crawling, battling to the gap. Most were caught in the crush, but a few succeeded in their frantic bid for freedom.

Two who succeeded were Fitzpatrick and Plumas.

Jessie had been keeping her eyes sharp for the trading-post owner, and had caught flashing glimpses of his girth during the conflict. Now, for the first time, she saw Fitzpatrick, accompanied by the traitorous aide Plumas, spurring horses out of the defile. Sheriff Maxwell was busy fighting over by the shaft house, too far from Jessie for her to signal. And Ki—she'd not been able to spot hide nor hair of him or Dion Nettle, much to her consternation and adding impetus to her rage to catch Fitzpatrick and Plumas. But Pierce Thorleigh chanced to be nearby, and he, too, noticed their escape.

"That fat bastard's making a break!" Thorleigh shouted, wrenching his horse about. Perversely, Jessie's mare shied mincingly, helping Fitzpatrick and Plumas by causing her to waste precious moments. Regaining control, she set off in hot pursuit, Thorleigh galloping a pace behind.

Through the pass and around the dogleg bulge they sped, lashing their mounts faster down the wagon trail, glimpsing Fitzpatrick and Plumas far ahead. Their quarry vanished over a distant crest. On they chased, though their horses were panting with raspy, harsh breaths.

Another rise, and again Jessie and Thorleigh spotted the fleeing duo and realized they were losing ground to them. Those other mounts were fresher, more rested, while theirs were winded from a long night of riding. And again the two ahead dipped down the opposite side of the sag and disappeared for quite a long distance, the trail curving through gullied slopes and wooded ledges.

The outlaws next came into view when they crossed an open patch of meadow. Jessie snapped a quick shot at Fitzpatrick. Her bullet whined past his head, making him flinch. He swiveled around and fired back. Plumas fired as well, their shots all flying wild. Jessie and Thorleigh raced after them along the trail, ignoring the bullets zinging past them, firing salvoes from their carbines, but their aim was no better than anyone's could be when shooting from the back of a galloping horse. Their mounts were flagging, still game, but simply too tuckered to keep up the grueling pace. Yet they refused to give in, determined to run to ground two leaders of the gang that had been terrorizing the region. Fitzpatrick and Plumas must not escape.

And then it was too late. The outlaws, hunching so low across their horses' withers that they were almost invisible, swerved around the bend at the far end of the meadow and dropped from sight behind a blocking wedge of trees.

Jessie and Thorleigh gave all their attention to riding. Her mare stumbled, recovered, and took the bend at an ungainly run. Thorleigh's horse was slowing to a ragged lope.

As they rounded the bend and the trail straightened again, Jessie yanked on her reins, pulling her horse to a sliding, staggering halt; behind her, Thorleigh did the same. Directly ahead, Fitzgerald and Plumas sat their blowing horses, Fitzgerald with his pistol out and Plumas with his shotgun leveled, black muzzles lined with her chest. And they were squeezing triggers.

Why the pair had decided to make a stand then and there, Jessie could not understand. Nor did she hold up her hand to ask. Her instant reaction was to figure Plumas as the more dangerous of them, what with his long-barreled shotgun, so she concentrated on him. She shot him five times with her pistol, shot him as she had never shot a man before. The enclosing timber pounded and hammered with gunshots, but it was as though she were stone-deaf; her ears simply didn't register them. Jessie, as if in a trance, watched Plumas tumble from his saddle in a tangle of lifeless arms and legs, roll, and become caught up under his horse's panic-kicking hooves.

But she did feel lead from Fitzpatrick's pistol rip through her hat. Thorleigh gave a half-twisting lurch as if grazed along the hip or over the ribs. Dimly, as if in a dream, she heard Thorleigh muttering through gritted teeth, "Don't forget, if you're in a terrible hurry, right above the belt buckle is the place." He didn't seem to be in a terrible hurry; he sat straight and targeted Fitzpatrick with deliberate care. As he pulled the trigger, he added, "It's your safety shot." Indeed it was. Pierce Thorleigh's diligent aim snatched the fat trader off his horse like he was axed, the bullet catching some bone inside and slipping up into his heart. He landed on his rump, his head wobbling as if shaking to deny he was dead.

Jessie glanced over at Thorleigh. "You all right?"

"Dandy, just peachy keen," he answered, holding his ribs. "It's only a flesh wound. Nothin' special."

"I'll have a look at it anyway," she said. "And thanks for nailing Fitzpatrick. I didn't know you could face fire and shoot so well."

"Neither did I. Never had to do it before, but I just had to rec'lect what I'd learned," he explained, glancing down at the blood oozing from his torn shirt. "She knew what she was talking about, Mom did."

Jessie ripped Thorleigh's shirt into strips to wrap his ribcage in a makeshift bandage. Then, tying the bodies across saddles, they set out back to the basin. They were relieved to find that Ki and Dion Nettle had survived the fray. Sheriff

Maxwell had knotted a kerchief around a bullet furrow in his scalp, and was hobbling about, searching for a boot heel that had been shot off. The able-bodied jacks were tending the wounded crewmen as well as the wounded gunmen, the rest of the gang having either died or vamoosed.

Nettle was rambling on under the stress of emotion at his rescue. He appeared to want to tell his entire experiences since the outlaws had caught him, as if fearful he wouldn't have another chance.

"The rats caught us in that clearing when we didn't have any idea of it, and shot the others down without a chance, in cold blood," he said hastily. Then his eyes suddenly gleamed. "Took me alive, but I almost got away from 'em right at first—almost. I kicked the hoss of the skunk that was riding alongside me, watching me, just before we reached Cedar Creek on the way here. When the hoss started to buck, I lit out lickety-split. Nothin' to do, though, but cross the creek, but no more'n I hit the water when a rope sings out, and I got pulled out of the creek like a moose out of a boghole. The next I knew I was here—been here ever since."

"You won't be much longer, pal," Thorleigh said cheerfully, grinning broadly. "You look a mess, though. P'raps you wouldn't mind waiting long enough to clean up before we ride back to camp—and Miz Opal."

Nettle brightened. "How is she, Pierce?"

"She's fine! As you may've guessed, plenty of folks broke legs jumping to the conclusion that you'd gone bad, killed your pards and stolen the payroll. But Miz Opal stuck by you. Well, you'll learn all that and everythin' else later."

"I wouldn't mind learnin' a tad more of everything," Maxwell complained, sitting on the ground as he tried to wedge his boot heel back on. "We got a passel of prisoners who might have something to say. And when we get back to town, I'm organizing the biggest posse this county has ever dreamed of. Give me half a day, and we'll catch up with the drivers of them ore-wagons before they can roll much farther. Give me all day, and any owlhoots out raidin' now will either be dead or fled. Mostly fled, I reckon. Scum working from order to order are disinclined to battle stubbornly over something they no longer can get. But dang me if I can make sense of precisely what's here they found so all-fired precious to get!"

"I think I might be able to help on that score," Jessie said, as she examined a chunk of black rock. Upon her return, she had gone over to where the ore-wagons had been loaded and scouted around for loose samples of what had been bagged in the gunnysacks. Now she handed the dark lump to Maxwell, adding, "Yes, and now I think I know why that trapper, Able Bone, was murdered. He must've stumbled onto this coal deposit."

"Coal!" Maxwell blurted disgustedly. "Now see here, Miz—"

"Not just any coal, Sheriff. You yourself told me the chief fields are in King County, but there it's all lignite coal—brownish, and slakes into powder when exposed to air. But see? This coal is a dull black, friable, and doesn't fragment easily."

"So what?"

"So it's my guess this's bituminous coal. It probably falls somewhere between middle-grade, which is good for the production of metallurgical dense coke; and low-grade bituminous, which is an ideal coal for steam locomotives. I've never heard of this variety in the Pacific Coast area, and believe me, if I had, Starbuck would've been in here fast, buying rights. Why, if this's the only deposit in the Territory, and the Northern Pacific is going to run track hereabouts, the Delmonicos own better than a gold mine!"

"Yeah . . ." Maxwell regarded the lump with newfound appreciation. "And t'waz Toad-Eye Topes who told us that Able Bone was a prospector at heart, reared in the Appalachians. I reckon Bone teethed on coal! They had to kill him, once they knew he knew."

"Somehow, Fitzpatrick or Locke discovered the coal's value," Jessie went on. "To get it, they set out to cause a feud between trappers and loggers to keep folks away and suspicion off them, and in the process tried to wreck the Delmonicos so they could get the land cheap. All the time they were making considerable easy money from mining and shipping the coal out, I imagine to buyers in Seattle or Tacoma. Smart, they were—too smart by half."

"Well, that practically winds things up," Maxwell declared. "We'll jug the gunnies and then arrest Locke and Lysander, him and his li'l black book. I prophesy with them and that telltale book, we'll know all the answers."

• • •

Maxwell's prediction came true. As soon as Urias Locke was picked up, he squealed like a stuck pig. Sherwin Lysander was caught napping, literally, and surrendered himself and his book without a struggle. Reading the entries, Jessie was astounded that the steer Yachats Sheales had given them would end in so rich a find. Lysander was a careful and accurate bookkeeper.

"But why," she asked Ki, "would any man, in a racket like this, put things in writing? His head's the only safe place for records of coal sales, or for what was paid the hired gunmen."

Ki shrugged. "Maybe he had to keep it for somebody else."

Jessie stared at Ki for a thoughtful moment. "That's it! And Lysander had good grounds for thinking it was safe enough. Only a few knew of its existence, and they were all in it. It would've been safe, too, if Sheales hadn't had an attack of conscience."

Jessie read on. She found a few names there that she was not happy to see, men with good reputations who had been unable to resist the temptation of a little easy money on the side. But nowhere in the book could she get even a hint of the thing she wanted to know. "I can't believe this whole show was Lysander's, and it doesn't make sense for Fitzpatrick and Locke to be listed in it if they're the ones Lysander was keeping it for. Wa-ait a minute . . ." She smiled at Ki, a satisfied smile indicating she'd figured it out. "Now all we need is a word with Sheriff Maxwell so he won't go scaring our bird into flight . . ."

Puyallup was a town with a history, a wild history. Gilroy Witherspoon, manager of the Puyallup branch of the Puget Sound Trust & Savings Bank, had seen some fairly hair-raising spectacles in his eighteen years there. But never had he seen anything that quite matched the red-faced, bristling-whiskered, thunder-eyed man who flung open the door to his office at one o'clock in the afternoon, accompanied by a beautiful young woman and an Asian gentleman.

This apparition, which had practically paralyzed the outer officers, slammed shut the door and sank into a chair, flanked by his two companions. Witherspoon, gray brows arching, got to his feet.

"Quinn Abbott! What in—"

Abbott made an imperative gesture. "Witherspoon, I ain't got much time. Park your carcass and listen!"

Twenty-three minutes later—the banker's secretary vouched for the time—the broker T. Horace Mahoney walked into the office. Mahoney was a short, stiff-featured man with odd, filmy gray eyes. In a harsh tone, he began, "I don't understand, Mr. Witherspoon, what all this rush is for—" Then he saw Abbott and friends, hesitated in perplexity, then demanded harshly, "Is this more of your incompetence, you dolt—"

The "dolt" rose and looked Mahoney over carefully. Mahoney stared at the anger-gnarled features. Then he made his mistake. Something in the scowl, in the hostility of the eyes—His hand flashed to his jacket.

"Hold it!"

The hand froze halfway as Ki gripped his arm. "Let go; let go!" Mahoney barked, struggling to no avail as Ki searched him, then tossed a hideaway pistol onto Witherspoon's desk.

"Wear it the same place Fitzpatrick did his, don't you?" Ki said conversationally, bending Mahoney's arm to force the man to sit down. "Now, stay put. This may take awhile."

Everybody settled in chairs.

Abbott growled, "Smoked you out at last!"

Mahoney glared, but fear had begun to creep into his anger.

Jessie spoke up, her voice cool and collected. "Fitzpatrick is dead, Mr. Mahoney. So is Plumas. They were killed resisting arrest, but I see you already know about that. Urias Locke is a prisoner. Also a double-crossing agent named Sherwin Lysander, and we have his little black account book."

Mahoney started to his feet, looked at Ki, and sank back.

"Stop me if we're wrong," Jessie said. "When you engineered the Northern Pacific buyout with Abbott, Fitzpatrick, and Locke, you persuaded Fitzpatrick and Locke to agree by intimating you weren't beyond playing fast and loose, if the money was right. So when Fitzpatrick and Locke needed a broker to sell their stolen coal, they came to you. A real cozy partnership. Then you saw another way to turn a dishonest dollar, and make shipping the coal safer from discovery. You'd buy up the Flaming Geyser line, and stall the sale to the N.P. as long as you could, while you transported coal to buyers all over the region, right out in the open. Of course, you couldn't turn the profit you wanted if you bought Flaming Geyser at a fair price—the price N.P. agreed to pay. So you got Fitzpatrick and Locke to use their raiders to ruin the business. Then you informed Abbott of your intentions, claiming those were Northern Pacific's intentions—to buy him out at half price—too late, you thought, for Abbott to catch on or help himself."

While Jessie was talking, laying out the scheme, Abbott studied Mahoney's white, working face before him, the staring, filmy eyes. When Jessie finished, Abbott said, "Do you know what I'm gonna do to you, Mahoney? I'm not pressing charges. No. I'm selling you my line. You'll pay the price originally agreed upon by the Northern Pacific."

The badgered Mahoney at last broke the silence that had been his best defense. "Damned if I will! You can't get away with this, any of you. You're running a bluff! Where's your evidence? You haven't—"

"The evidence," Jessie cut in, "is all ready to be presented in court. Oh, and I'll pursue it for Abbott with the best detectives, the best legal advice money can buy, for as long as it takes to send you up."

"She means it, Mahoney. And she's heeled. You're not only tangling with me, but with Miz Jessica Starbuck, *the* Starbuck of *the* Starbuck,"

Abbott declared. "Shall I raise the ante? Or do you prefer the penitentiary?"

Mahoney said between his teeth, "Okay, you leech. I'll buy!"

"And figure," Abbott asked softly, "on making up the difference out of the country, the way you've been doing? Oh, no, Mahoney. You buy this line and sell it honestly to the N.P. or run it straight. But if there's ever a whisper of dirty dealing, behind the bars you go. The evidence will still be good."

Mahoney's jaws were stiff. "Your proposition's impossible, on the face of it! How can I make a living out of your line, after this?"

Abbott didn't get the force of the question, and it was Gilroy Witherspoon who explained. "He means when all this comes out, Mr. Abbott."

"Oh! But it won't come out, Mahoney."

"Do—do you mean," Mahoney stammered, "that you're not going to give the whole thing away?"

"Not if you come across."

"But why?"

"Because there're a lot of loyal employees who're working for me, and I want to see them continue to work in good jobs for good wages. And a railroad that's going to make a big difference in the lives of everyone up in that part of the county, and I'd hate to see those plans derailed. Just chalk it up to being good for good folks, somethin' you aren't ever likely to figure out. Is it a deal?"

Mahoney was whipped and looked it. "Yes."

"Make out the check to this bank." When it was written, Abbott endorsed it and handed it to Witherspoon. "The bank can draw up the necessary papers, both for the sale to Mahoney and the clearance of my loan."

Witherspoon rose to shake hands. "And you, Mr. Abbott?"

"Me?" Abbott glanced at Jessie and Ki, grinning. "Why, I reckon we're going out to collect a certain field agent named Gresham, and then sit around the fanciest meal to be found in town, discussin' potential new business deals."

Watch for

LONE STAR AND THE NEVADA GOLD

147th in the exciting LONE STAR series
from Jove

Coming in November!